"You're trying too hard to remember, Luc,"

Alison said, her tone sympathetic to his frustration. "Sometimes, memories come when you least expect them."

Luc turned around to face her. Something was nudging a thought in his mind. But it was shimmering just out of reach.

"Yeah, maybe you're right," he said finally.

He saw her smile and immediately felt something stir inside him in response. The smile was sensual, but innocent at the same time. More questions came to mind, but this time they had to do with her.

Maybe she was the missing link—not just to his memory, but to his heart....

Marie Ferrarella

Found: His Perfect Wife

Published by Silhouette Books
America's Publisher of Contemporary Romance

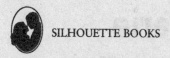

SILHOUETTE BOOKS

ISBN 0-373-36005-3

FOUND: HIS PERFECT WIFE

Visit Silhouette Books at www.eHarlequin.com

Printed in U.S.A.

MARIE FERRARELLA

USA TODAY bestselling author Marie Ferrarella began writing when she was eleven. She began selling many years after that. Along the way, she acquired a master's in Shakespearean comedy, a husband and two kids (in that order)—the dog came later. She sold her first romance in November of 1981. The road from here to there has 155 more sales to it, with 144 being to Harlequin. She has received several RITA® Award nominations over the years with one win for *Father Goose* (in the Traditional category). Marie figures she will be found one day—many, many years from now—slumped over her computer, writing to the last moment with a smile on her face.

To Jessi with love, Mom

Prologue

Terrific, just terrific.

For the first time in a very long time, he felt like having a drink. But that wouldn't help anything. It was because he'd taken a drink—several drinks—that he was in this predicament to begin with.

"Bad news?"

Luc LeBlanc looked over his shoulder to see his cousin Ike standing behind him. The Salty, the saloon they both owned and Ike ran, was nearly empty this time of day.

Ike had been watching his cousin for a while now. He indicated the letter lying on the table in front of him.

Luc drew the letter closer to him. "What makes you ask that?"

"The vein in your neck looked like it was going to pop out just then." Without waiting to be invited, Ike turned the letter toward him and scanned the contents.

They were closer than brothers and there were no secrets between them. For that matter, there were precious few in a town the size of Hades. It was average only by Alaskan standards. Coming to the portion that had Luc silently swearing, Ike raised his eyes to look at his cousin. "Wow, what makes Jacob think you're—?"

"Married?" Luc shrugged, looking off. "Might have been something I said when I ran into him in Anchorage."

"Well, if you want to save face, looks like you might have to go on a wife hunt." Ike grinned. "I'd lend you mine but I'm just getting the hang of being a husband myself and I might lose my place if I let you borrow Marta for appearance's sake." He grew serious. "What are you going to do?"

Luc stared down at the letter. "I don't know."

"This," Ike said as he got up to get the bar ready for the mine workers who came in to the Salty Saloon at noon, "is going to be interesting."

Interesting wouldn't have been the word he would have used, Luc thought. Frustration surged through him. He resisted the urge to crumple the letter. Crumpling it wouldn't make the problem go away. It was coming via an airplane in a little more than three weeks. Both of them were coming.

Served him right. He'd lied; now he was going to have to pay for it. Which meant owning up to the truth.

Something he wasn't looking forward to.

He'd lived with and by the truth all his life, not fanatically, but just because it was his way. To his recollection, the lie he'd allowed to slip out in a moment of pure, unadulterated weakness had been the only one he'd ever told.

People lied every day, even here in Hades. Especially

here in Hades, he thought, where boredom almost demanded it. It was a form of creative art in this tiny town hovering a hundred miles away from Anchorage. None of the townsfolk had probably ever had to face up to the fact that they had lied to someone who had once, when life was simpler, been their best friend.

But he had lied to Jacob and now he was going to have to admit it.

What he needed, Luc decided, wasn't a drink. It was to get away. Both were only temporary fixes, but a trip would do him far more good than alcohol. Maybe now was the time for that visit to Seattle he'd been promising himself.

He rolled it over in his head. Seattle. Sure, why not?

It might just be the thing to help him pull his thoughts together and figure out how to handle this without completely humiliating himself.

Chapter One

The indignant scream sliced through his thoughts like a newly honed scalpel.

By the time the angry barrage of words had followed in the scream's wake, Jean-Luc LeBlanc had already whirled around on his heel and was running to the rescue. The reaction was purely instinctive, without so much as a shred of thought on his part to slow him down. Certainly it didn't occur to him that a threat here on the streets of Seattle was something quite different from a threat in Hades, Alaska. There, more than likely, danger came from four-legged creatures or merciless weather. In the lower forty-nine, danger walked on two legs and could be just as merciless as any act of nature. Sometimes even more.

Luc didn't stop to reason out anything, or weigh pros and cons. None of that mattered. Someone needed help and Luc was close by. That was enough for him.

It took only a moment to orient himself. Behind him in the alley, the taxi driver—who'd picked him up at the airport and had just, less than half a minute earlier, dropped him off near the hotel where he would be staying—was fighting someone off. The attacker was in the front seat of the cab, grappling with her. Something flashed, catching the light.

The man had a knife.

Luc threw aside his suitcase, running faster. "Let her go!"

The voice, deep and dangerous, seemed almost incongruous with his open, blond good looks. But he had the build and the muscles to back up the warning in his voice. Reaching the cab, Luc grabbed the would-be mugger by the back of the neck and roughly hauled him out. He threw the mugger aside as if the man was nothing more than an undesirable, miserable rag.

Caught by surprise, the man's knife flew out of his hand. He went crashing into the broad side of a Dumpster housed against the rear of a tall building opposite the back of the hotel. Luc could almost feel the man's brains rattling as his head made contact with the metal side.

His eyes still on the mugger, Luc stooped to pick up the fallen knife, meaning to toss it out of play.

Shrieking a curse that was almost intelligible, the mugger scrambled to his feet and lunged himself at Luc. Rather than throw it, Luc could only kick the knife aside. With the wind knocked out of him, Luc still managed to gain his feet quickly. He raised his fists to defend himself the way he'd learned when he was barely into his teens.

Luc heard the cabdriver yell and realized a heartbeat later that it was a warning. The warning melded with the sudden, excruciating pain crashing down on his skull.

And then everything went black.

Damn it, she shouldn't have parked here.

She should have known better. But the street out in front of the Embassy Hotel was being torn up in both directions. The ongoing reconstruction of MacArthur Boulevard had forced her to pull the cab around to an alley that was best left to inhabitants of the night and to burly deliverymen driving large trucks. The alley certainly wasn't any place for a recently graduated nursing student who drove her brother's taxi in an attempt to earn a little money.

One eye on the fight, her heart pounding double time, Alison Quintano looked frantically around for a patrol car, but there was none in sight. It figured.

Swearing, she grabbed the lid of a trash can and hurled it at the second mugger who had appeared out of nowhere. The arm that had her older brothers swearing should have belonged to a first draft baseball rookie remained true and she clipped the second mugger on the back of the head, throwing him off balance. But not before the man had knocked out her recent fare.

Fury was in the man's eyes as he swung around. Reflexes had him clutching at the back of his head. When he looked at his hand, there was blood. "Son of a bitch, I'm going to make you pay for that."

He started after her, only to have his partner yell at him. "Ain't got time for that." He rifled through the prone man's pockets. "We've gotta get out of here!"

The second mugger looked torn. Common sense prevailed and he followed the first man, stopping only to grab the fallen suitcase. Running down the alley, they disappeared.

Alison fought back the desire to chase after them. That would be stupid. There wasn't anything she could do. Besides, there were two of them, and while not big, they could still easily overpower her. Look what they had done to her fare.

Abandoning the thought of pursuit, she hurried over to her Good Samaritan.

The man was flat on his stomach.

She got a sick feeling in hers.

Dropping to her knees, she placed her fingertips to the side of his neck. A pulse. She released the breath that had gotten clogged in her lungs at the sight of his unconscious body.

He was alive, but out cold. The second mugger had come up on him from behind, hitting him over the head with what looked like a kid's bat. How much damage was there? Very gently she rolled the man onto his back. Gingerly she pried apart his eyelids one at a time. His pupils didn't appear to be dilated, but that could still change.

Except for one cut over his left eye and what looked like the beginning of a nasty bruise on his cheek, it looked as if her Good Samaritan hadn't been too seriously hurt.

She hoped.

Placing her hand lightly on his shoulder, she gently tried to rouse him without success.

"Are you all right?" She leaned in closer so that he could hear her. "Mister, can you hear me? Are you all right?"

He lay still and unresponsive.

This wasn't good.

Worried, Alison looked around, but there was absolutely no one walking by the alley's opening. Murphy's Law. It seemed almost impossible, given that she was practically in the heart of Seattle.

For a second, she debated trying to wake him again. Maybe she should just go for help. To do the latter, she'd have to leave him and she was reluctant. He was unconscious and couldn't defend himself, and while crime didn't exactly run rampant in the streets, they had just been mugged. She didn't want to take any more chances. The man was unconscious and that made him her responsibility.

Alison settled on trying to raise her brother on the two-way radio in the cab. She glanced at her watch. Almost two, but it was still considered lunchtime by a few. If she had any sort of luck left, Kevin should still be in his office.

This was going to make her brother blow his top, she thought. He hadn't been keen on her taking the part-time position to begin with, never mind that it was with the cab company he owned. She was the baby of the family and everyone was always being protective of her.

Except once, but that had been no one's fault.

Right now, she was far more concerned with her Good Samaritan than her brother's reaction. She'd deal with that later. As she began to rise, she saw the man's eyes flutter slightly.

He was coming around.

The next second, he opened his eyes. She hadn't realized, when she'd glanced back at him in her rearview mirror earlier, just how blue his eyes were.

Alison sucked in air, and then exhaled it again, in almost a sigh of relief.

"You're awake." Relief was short-lived as her train-

ing reared its head again. Just because his eyes were
open didn't mean he was all right—not by a long shot.
Sympathy flooded her. At the very least, the man had to
have one mother of a headache. "How do you feel? That
was some wallop he gave you."

It took him a second to realize she was talking to him.
He'd been too mesmerized by what he saw to absorb
any of the words. He'd opened his eyes to find himself
looking up at an angel. An angel with an abundance of
dark, chestnut-colored wavy hair and eyes the color of
the sky that was above her head.

She was talking about someone hitting him. "Who?"

He looked a little disoriented. Under the circumstances she couldn't blame him. "The mugger."

"Mugger?" He struggled to sit up, feeling as if there
was an anvil on his forehead.

Maybe he hadn't put two and two together yet, she
thought. Taking his hand, she slowly helped him into a
sitting position, watching his face carefully. "Yeah,
there was another one."

He was trying to make sense of what she was saying
to him and having very little luck. "Another one."

The unease slowly began to return. "Why are you
repeating everything I say?"

Luc passed a hand over his forehead. "Just trying to
get a clear picture in my mind."

Or any picture, he thought. God, but his head ached.
The pain was crowding out any thoughts he was trying
to grasp, squeezing them away.

Looking at his eyes, Alison sat back on her heels.
"Anybody would be muddled after going through what
you just did." The blank look on his face had her adding, "Coming to my rescue like that was nothing short
of sheer bravery." Something straight out of King Ar-

thur, her favorite section of literature. She smiled at him. "Don't see much of that these days." Guilt began to nibble at her again. He did look rather out of it. "Sorry you seemed to have gotten the worst of it. I beamed the second guy with a garbage can lid, but it didn't seem to hurt him very much. Man probably had a head made out of stone, which would be in keeping with his Neanderthal behavior." And then she smiled at her rescuer. "Not like you."

He was trying, but he just wasn't following any of this. "Not like me what?"

"Hurting him. I didn't hurt him the way you did the other guy." Now she was really concerned. She looked at him more closely. Her initial impression held. His pupils hadn't dilated, but that didn't mean they were out of the woods. "Are you sure you're all right?"

The pounding in his head was beginning to jar his teeth. "I don't know. I'm not exactly sure what all right is."

Oh, God. Anxious now, Alison held up her hand in front of him.

"How many fingers am I holding up?" When he didn't answer immediately, she moved her hand back and forth until she secured his attention. "How many do you see?"

Luc blinked, but even that seemed to bring about an avalanche thundering in his brain. It took effort to speak. "Two, you're holding up two fingers. When you're not wiggling them."

"Good number. Could be a guess," she added under her breath. She tried something else. "Do you know what day it is?"

He thought for a long moment, then looked at her. "No."

Don't jump to conclusions. It's not bad yet, she told herself. There were times, when she was very busy, that she lost track of the days, as well. Still, the uneasiness was building within her. "It's Wednesday. Do you know where you are?"

Though it hurt to move his head, he looked around very slowly. The street was narrow and there were two tall buildings vying for the sky. A distant smell of something rotting drifted toward him. "An alley?"

Alison suppressed the sigh before it could escape. This was looking worse by the second. "Nothing more than that?"

He looked again, this time moving only his eyes. it hurt less that way. "A dirty alley?"

Batting zero. She leaned in closer. "Do you know who I am?"

Her name, along with a license number, was on the back of the front seat. She remembered he'd read it out loud once he'd given her the address of the hotel, commenting that it was pretty. There had been a short, pleasant conversation about nothing on the drive over here.

He paused now before answering. Was she someone important to him? He had a feeling that she might be, but it was nothing that he could actually put into words. "A beautiful woman?"

The answer immediately dredged up suspicions. Was this all a ruse? Was he just trying to hit on her? He had gotten a blow to his head, but maybe he was all right and just milking the incident to elicit sympathy from her and possibly something more.

She sat back on her heels, straightening. "Is this a trick?"

"No, no trick." He pressed fingertips to his head, wishing he could somehow push back the all-encompassing pain. "Unless you're doing it with mirrors." He winced suddenly as the pain seemed to spike upward, all but piercing his skull.

Falling back on professionalism, Alison examined the back of his head more closely. There was no blood, thank God. Still, that didn't mean that there wasn't something going on internally. He needed to be seen by a doctor, the sooner the better.

She sighed again, this time exasperated with the situation.

"No mirrors," she answered. "Just what do you remember?"

He tried to think, but there was a low-grade buzzing in his ears and it made it hard to knit any words together, never mind forming a coherent reply.

After a frustrating moment, he raised his eyes to hers. "Nothing."

The single-word answer felt like a bullet that had gone straight to her chest. This was her fault. She should have taken her chances with the construction and just let him off in the middle of the block. But she had been in a hurry and had wanted to get to her next fare.

She struggled against the implications that were staring her in the face. "Nothing? What d'you mean, nothing?"

His eyes held hers. She sounded concerned. *Who are you? Are we lovers? Friends?* Fragments of questions came and went, leaving small, colored trails through his head, which led nowhere.

"I don't remember anything. It's all…just a blur." There was wonder in his voice, as if he was discovering all this for the first time as well. Discovering it and being appalled at the same time.

"You don't remember where you came from?" She

knew what he was saying, yet she had to say it all out loud for herself, stalling for time. Hoping it would all return to him in a flash and absolve her of the responsibility she felt.

He paused and tried to think again. There was nothing. Except defeat. "No."

He'd given her the hotel's address. Maybe he was meeting someone there. At least it was a place to start. "How about where you were going?"

This time, the negative reply came accompanied with a sigh that was both weary and frustrated. "No."

With effort, she drew on what she'd been taught, plus an inherent way of being able to comfort everyone but herself. Her voice was calm, displaying none of the sympathetic panic she was experiencing for the stranger at her feet.

"Your name…can you remember your name?"

There was something, hovering just out of reach, but when he tried to capture it, it broke apart into a thousand tiny pieces, like confetti blowing away in the wind.

"No."

And then she remembered. He'd mentioned his name to her just after he'd said hers. He made a joke about not having the time to wait for a formal introduction. At the time it had struck her that he was incredibly friendly. She wasn't accustomed to friendly, not off the campus. People generally kept to themselves in this part of the city, more concerned with where they were going and how fast they could get there.

She thought now. It was John something. No, wait, Jean-Luc, that was it.

She looked at him eagerly, hoping this was the trigger that would start the process rolling. She knew it could be as simple a thing as that, just a word, a look.

"Does the name Jean-Luc sound familiar?"

Though it hurt, he tried to fit the name to himself, waiting for a flash of recognition. Of another name that might attach itself to the first.

But there was nothing.

The only thing he recalled seemed strange and out of context. "Wasn't there a science-fiction program on with—?"

It had been something she'd said to him when he'd told her his name. *That* he remembered. Alison banked down her impatience, knowing it was really directed at the situation, not the man.

"Yes. *Star Trek, the Next Generation.* Captain Jean-Luc Picard." Repeating the information she'd originally given him verbatim, Alison waited for a sign of some sort of recognition in his eyes.

Nothing.

Either the man was an accomplished actor, or he really did have amnesia.

Amnesia. It was an ugly word.

He tried to resist the disorientation. Like quicksand, it only sucked him in deeper. Looking at her, he felt around his pockets. "Shouldn't I have some sort of identification on me?"

He really *didn't* remember the mugging, she thought. Otherwise he'd know. "They took it from you." She'd seen the first mugger quickly go through Jean-Luc's pockets after he went down.

"They?" With effort, struggling for at least an island of sense within this murky sea, he connected two of the myriad of dots floating through his head. "You mean the muggers?"

"Yes." Alison looked over her shoulder toward the cab. Three of its doors were still hanging open, ponderous wings unable to lift something so heavy. "I think you'd probably be more comfortable in the cab." She bit her lip, her eyes sweeping over him. "Do you think you can get up?"

"Let's see." It seemed like a simple enough question and an even more simple enough feat to execute under normal circumstances.

But when he attempted to do it, the world decided to remain just where it had been a second ago and not make the journey with him.

Instead, it spun around in a mad whirl, mixing colors and buildings all together. Trying desperately to hang on to stability, he still felt himself losing his grasp on his surroundings. Clutching at air, he wound up grabbing at Alison instead.

Oh, God, he was going to fall, Alison realized a second before he grabbed her shoulder. Quickly her arms surrounded him and she felt her knees buckling under the unexpected weight. Contact had her involuntarily stiffening. Remembering.

She forbid herself to go there. "Lean on me," she ordered through clenched teeth.

It was a miracle they didn't both fall over. At the last second, in an attempt to compensate for the shift in balance, she braced her legs, planting them farther apart, like a weight lifter going for a world-class record.

"Whoa, you're more solid than you look," she gasped. For a second, it was touch and go whether or not they would both land on the pavement.

He felt her breath against his face, felt the heat of her body as she struggled not to be thrown off balance. The sound of her heavy breathing penetrated the fog descending on his brain. With effort, he chased away the darkness encroaching on him.

"Sorry." A line of perspiration formed along his brow and between his shoulder blades as he struggled to regain his equilibrium.

"Not your fault." Still braced, testing the waters slowly, she began to release her hold on him. The stiffness within her was harder to release. "I'm the one who should be sorry."

"For what?" She felt soft, enticingly soft. The thought pushed its way in through the clutter of pain that insisted on holding him prisoner. It was a tiny bit of sanctuary within a world engulfed in chaos.

"If you hadn't come to my rescue, you wouldn't have made intimate contact with the cement. Who knows what they could have done if you hadn't come along." Despite herself, she shivered. It took everything she had not to allow the memory to return, to hold her hostage. There was no time for that. She couldn't let it get the upper hand on her. Not again. "You don't remember anything, do you?"

His hand on her shoulder to prevent another embarrassing dip, he walked slowly to the cab.

"No, I don't." He looked at her, his head pounding. "But if I came to your rescue, I'm glad, even if it did cause everything to disappear." Concern entered his eyes. "Did they hurt you?"

He was asking about her. His memory had been reduced to that of an eggplant because of her and he was still asking if she was hurt. She couldn't make up her mind if he was for real or a figment of her imagination.

"They didn't have time. You were too quick."

He lowered himself into the back seat, his legs giving out at the last minute. What had that guy hit him with, anyway?

"I don't feel very quick now," he confessed. He stopped, considering. "Jean-Luc, huh?"

"That's what you said." She remembered something else. "But you added that everyone calls you Luc."

"Luke." He rolled the name over in his mind, waiting for a familiar ring. And then something seemed to gel. "Luc," he said suddenly. "It's not Luke, it's Luc."

She heard no difference, but as long as it made one to him, that was all that mattered. She looked at him eagerly, not wanting this man's condition on her conscience. She had just attained her life's dream of becoming a nurse. That meant helping people, not putting them in harm's way. "Do you remember?"

He knew she meant more. But there was only that. "Just that Luc is my name."

She wasn't about to give up easily. "Luc what?" she prodded.

He tried, he really tried, but nothing came. Trying to move his head from side to side, he instantly aborted the effort, regretting it. "I haven't got the vaguest clue."

Chapter Two

Detective John Donnelley stared at his notepad. Twenty-five minutes of questioning had resulted in less than half a page of writing. It was hot and muggy and he was struggling to keep his irritability from showing. Passing his hand over a near-bald pate that had once sported more than its share of hair, he shook his head.

"Not much to go on." He looked at the man he'd been questioning as he flipped the book closed.

Alison resisted the urge to place herself between the two men. It was her natural mothering instinct coming to the fore, an instinct she'd acquired ever since her own mother had passed away over sixteen years ago.

"It all happened very fast," she interjected. Luc had been through enough, and in her estimation, he wasn't looking all that good right now. He didn't need to be grilled any longer. "Five minutes, tops. Probably more like three."

The bald head moved up and down slowly, thoughtfully. "Usually the way." Donnelley eyed Luc. The impression that Luc might be a suspect didn't appear to be entirely out of the detective's range of thought. "And there's nothing you can add?"

Luc tried to think, to summon a memory. Something. It was like trying to find angel food cake in a snowdrift. "'Fraid not."

Still, Donnelley pressed one more time. "Height, weight, coloring—?" Dark eyebrows rose high on an even higher forehead, waiting. Moderately hopeful.

There was no point in pretending. "I wouldn't know them if they were part of that crowd," Luc admitted honestly, gesturing toward the people who had gathered behind the sawhorses that defined the crime scene, separating it from the rest of the alley.

Why was the man going over the same thing again? Luc needed a doctor, not a badgering police detective who looked as if he was ten years past weary. "We've been through all that," Alison pointed out.

The protectiveness welled up within her. It would have been funny if she'd stopped to analyze it. She was slight, almost petite in comparison to Luc, yet she felt as if he needed her to run interference. At least until he was himself again. Whoever that was.

"He told you, Detective, he can't remember anything that happened. Why do you keep asking him the same questions?"

The slight shrug wasn't a hundred percent convincing. "All I'm saying is that it seems awfully convenient, this loss of memory." His eyes met Luc's. Something within him relented. He could feel the girl's eyes boring into him. She seemed convinced enough for both of them, he thought. "Hey, listen, I'm just trying to do my job here. You don't push, you don't get answers, right?"

"Sometimes you don't get answers even when you do push," she replied quietly. But he was right, she supposed. The man had probably seen it all. Certainly far more than she ever had. That made everyone suspect in his eyes. Even her. She shrugged. "Sorry, it's just that he needs to see a doctor."

Donnelley looked at Luc's face. His pallor was almost ghostly. No point in beating a dead horse, at least for now.

"Okay, you can go," he told Luc. His voice was almost casual as he asked what sounded like an afterthought, "Where can we reach you, in case there's something else?"

Luc slipped his hands into his pockets. If there'd been money there originally, there was none now. His pockets were empty. All he had, as far as he knew, were the clothes on his back.

"I don't know."

Luc frowned. He was getting very sick of the sound of that. Perforce, it was his reply to almost everything. Because he didn't know. Didn't know his name, didn't know where he'd been or where he was going. Didn't even know how old he was or if there was someone waiting for him. Someone getting increasingly worried as the minutes slipped away.

Frustration ate away at him, filling up all the empty spaces.

The detective paused, considering. And then he reached back into his pocket for his notepad. Writing something down quickly, he tore off the page and held the single sheet out to Luc.

"Here's the address of a shelter in the area." Donnelley tried to distance himself from what he was saying. There was a hot meal waiting for him at the end of his shift. A hot meal and a good woman in a tidy, three-bedroom house he'd almost paid off. He wouldn't have liked to be in this kid's place now. "Cleaner than most. They can fix you up with a meal and a cot. Maybe it'll come back to you by morning." The note in his voice said he had his doubts.

Luc took the page. Standing on her toes, Alison managed to look over his shoulder at the address. It was an area she tried to avoid when she drove the cab. Her eyes met the detective's. "Not the best address."

Donnelley laughed shortly, avoiding Luc's eyes. "As a rule, rich people don't generally need shelters in their neighborhoods."

Right now, he didn't have the luxury of being choosy. Folding the sheet, Luc tucked it into his shirt pocket. "Thanks."

Alison was getting antsy. "And you have my number." It wasn't a question.

Donnelley held up his notepad. He'd written the information down on top of the page. "Right here."

She began to back away. Being the center of attention had never sat well with her, and the crowd kept growing rather than diminishing. "Then we can go?"

The detective gestured toward the taxicab. "Already said you could. Feel free."

Free was the last thing she felt, but it was all she needed to hear. "Let's go," she tossed over her shoulder at Luc.

For a second, he'd thought she was going to leave him behind. Apparently she thought of them as being in this together. He found that oddly comforting, considering that they apparently hadn't known each other before the fateful cab ride.

He followed behind her. But when he started to open the passenger door in the front, she looked at him in surprise. "What are you doing?"

He stopped. It seemed pretty clear to him. "Getting in."

Her eyes indicated the back seat. "Why aren't you getting in the back?" After all, that was where fares were supposed to ride. In the back. Away from her.

He hesitated, then decided to put the matter to her. "If you don't mind, I'd rather sit up front with you. I feel too isolated sitting back there." He'd sat there earlier, waiting for the police to arrive and there had been this pervading feeling of being cut off. He couldn't successfully deal with that right now.

Alison caught her bottom lip between her teeth. She didn't know if it was a line, or if he was being serious. She supposed it wouldn't do any harm. He looked far too unsteady to try anything in his present condition. And these were unusual circumstances.

"Okay," she murmured, getting in on her side. "You can ride up front."

Luc stared at the seat belt a full moment, as if analyzing it, before he slid the metal tongue into the groove. "Where are we going?"

Picking her way through the alley, she turned the car to the south and prayed for no traffic. "To get you checked out."

That was going to cost. "I don't have any money," he pointed out needlessly.

She flipped her blinker on, easing into the turn lane. "Don't worry, I know the doctor there."

* * *

The doctor she knew turned out to be an intern. And her brother. Alison knew for a fact that Jimmy, three and a half years her senior, was on call in the emergency room at University Medical Center. With any luck, Luc could be quickly walked through this ordeal.

And then what?

The question drummed through her head as she brought the taxi to a halt in the tiny lot.

And then, she told herself, she'd take it one step at a time. Who knew? Maybe he'd get his memory back by the time they walked out through the doors again.

She was on nodding terms with half the staff on duty during the early-afternoon shift. It was something she was counting on.

"We're here," she announced needlessly to Luc.

Getting out, trying not to move quicker than his head, Luc looked around. "Shouldn't we be going through the front?"

This was the back entrance, reserved for ambulances and paramedics. And the staff. "This is faster." She ushered Luc in through the electronic doors.

The receptionist glanced up from her book as Alison hurried by. Her fingers marking her place, she appeared vaguely annoyed at the sudden disturbance.

"Jimmy around, Julie?"

It took the young woman a couple of seconds before recognition set in. A smile followed. "Sure. He's in the lounge. Slow morning," she commented just before returning to her book.

"Not anymore," Alison muttered.

Realizing that Luc wasn't beside her any longer, she glanced over her shoulder. She'd lost him at the entrance. There were two nurses in front of him, question-

ing his presence. And just possibly, she observed, trying
to draw a little personal information from him, as well.

You're out of luck, girls.

Not that she could fault them for trying. Luc was definitely in the cute category, she allowed. Actually, she
decided, scrutinizing him, he was more than cute. A lot
more. Not that that was either here or there. At least, not
for her.

Retracing her steps, Alison planted herself between
the two nurses and Luc. She knew one of the women.
"Grace, I'm looking for Jimmy."

"In the lounge." Grace hardly spared her a glance.
"Anything we can do?" The question was directed at
Luc. "A sponge bath while you're waiting?"

Without thinking, only reacting, Alison laced her hand
through his and pulled Luc away. "He can give himself
his own bath."

Despite his condition, Luc couldn't help smiling.
"Are they always that friendly?"

She led him down a hallway whose walls were long
overdue for a painting. Cracked in a number of places,
the paint was beginning to peel here and there along the
perimeters.

"They usually don't have enough time to be that
friendly. Looks like you picked the right time to be
mugged."

He doubted if there was such a thing. At least, not
from the way his head was feeling.

"This way." Pushing open the unlocked door, she
called out to her brother. "Jimmy."

He looked like her, Luc thought, picking Jimmy Quintano out of the small cluster of men in green livery sitting or standing inside the stuffy room. They had the

same color chestnut hair, the same blue eyes and the same winking dimple in their right cheek.

Right now, Jimmy looked a good deal more indolent than his younger sister.

Half turning from the program he was watching on a small, beat-up television someone had donated to the cause, Jimmy leaned back in one of the chairs that framed the kitchen table, another donation.

"Hey, Aly, what's up?" He looked back at the screen. "I thought you were driving the cab today."

"I was." She would have preferred sharing this with him alone, but she couldn't always pick her locations. Besides, she knew how fast word spread within the infrastructure of the hospital's staff. "Until two guys decided they wanted the fare money."

The easy smile vanished. Jimmy was on his feet instantly, crossing to her. "You hurt?" Even as he asked, his eyes washed over her as he passed his hands over her arms.

"I'm okay, but I probably wouldn't have been if he hadn't come to my rescue." For the first time, Jimmy noticed that his sister hadn't come in alone. He wasn't accustomed to Alison being with a man. Not since her divorce. "Jimmy, this is Luc. Luc, my brother Jimmy Quintano."

A few of the others in the room clustered around them, silently giving their sympathy to Alison, respecting her space. Jimmy focused on Luc. Grateful, Jimmy grasped Luc's hand in both of his. "Hey, man, thanks. I mean it." Sincerity clouded his mind for a second. "I didn't catch your last name. Luc what?"

She wanted to spare Luc as much as possible. "That's part of the reason we're here," Alison told Jimmy.

He looked from Luc to his sister. "I don't understand."

Before Luc could say anything, Alison began explaining the situation to her brother.

"Luc can't remember anything. One of the muggers hit him from behind and he went down on the sidewalk." She indicated the gash on his forehead. "He hit his head. Hard. When he came to, he didn't know where he was. Or who."

Jimmy tried to fill in the blanks. "And I take it they took his ID."

She nodded. "Cleaned him out." Alison flashed an apologetic look at Luc. "Suitcase, wallet. Everything but the lint in his pockets."

Jimmy could hear the frustrated tone in his sister's voice. "Excuse me for a minute." Making his apology to Luc, he took Alison aside. "You're not to blame, you know."

Though she appreciated what he was trying to do, she'd always been willing to take responsibility for her own actions. And this was lying right at her doorstep. "He came to my rescue. He was defending me, Jimmy. If I'm not to blame, then who is?"

He knew she had more than enough to deal with as it was. He was careful not to show it, but he worried about Alison. They all did—he, Kevin and Lily. His younger sister was friendly and outgoing, but there'd always been this definite cut-off point for her past which she wouldn't allow men to venture. The only exception had been her husband. But that union had been short-lived, not lasting out a year. Ever since then, she'd become even more withdrawn than ever as far as her social life went.

There were times when he thought of her as a wounded sparrow. A hint of the very idea would have probably had her beating on him with both fists just to show him how unsparrowlike she was.

But he knew better. "Society, lax laws, the muggers—I can give you a list." His eyes were kind as he looked at her closely. "You sure they didn't hurt you?"

He'd look into her soul if he could, she knew that. But that was a closed area, even to him. "I'm sure. Just take care of Luc, all right? I really feel responsible for him, Jimmy."

"All right." Slipping his arm around her shoulders, Jimmy turned toward Luc. "Let's get that head X-rayed, Luc. Make sure there isn't something going on we should be aware of."

Jimmy shut off the back light and pulled the two X rays off the display. Alison had shadowed his every move, insisting on looking at the X rays herself. He knew that her goal was to become a nurse-practitioner, but he wished she would give him a little space right now.

Slipping the X rays into a large manila envelope, he looked at Luc. The news was excellent. "No evidence of any swelling. In my professional opinion, you just got banged up a bit."

"And the amnesia?" Alison pressed.

Since Luc and not his sister was the patient, Jimmy addressed his words to him. "Should clear up. Day or so." He paused, then qualified. "With luck."

"Should," Luc repeated slowly, absorbing the word into the vast abyss that existed in his mind. "But no guarantees."

Jimmy knew there was no way he could actually commiserate with his patient's situation. How would he have felt, waking up, finding his whole world erased? It was a scary thought. "Nothing in life is."

"Except death and taxes." Luc stopped abruptly to examine the line that had come to him out of the blue. He'd heard that somewhere. But where, when? He squelched down the frustration and concentrated, instead, on the fact that he had remembered something, no matter how trivial. Progress.

"Yeah." Jimmy made one final notation in Luc's chart before closing it. He wondered how the receptionist was going to file this, given that there was no last name. Her problem. "Except for that." Setting the chart aside, he picked up a small white packet and handed it to Luc. "I'm giving you ten pills. Take one every four hours for the pain if it gets too much. It'll make you sleepy," he warned, "but then, it doesn't look as if you're about to operate any heavy machinery in the immediate future."

Luc stared down at the packet before putting it away. "If it's all the same, I'd rather keep alert. My head's already fuzzy enough as it is."

Jimmy could empathize with that. Luc had described one killer of a headache. "Up to you." He paused, thinking. Without a clue as to who he was and with no money, Luc had nowhere to stay. "You know, there's a shelter not too far from here—" He began reaching for a pen and something to write on.

"He already has an address to a shelter," Alison cut in. "The police detective gave it to him." She had no firsthand knowledge of what one of those places looked like, but she'd watched a documentary. It was enough to help her make up her mind.

Jimmy missed the look in her eyes. "So I guess you're set."

"Looks like," Luc agreed.

"Thanks again for saving the runt." He nodded at Alison as he shook Luc's hand. "We've gotten used to having her around."

Luc had a feeling that he had no idea what to do with gratitude. At least, he didn't know how to respond now, so he merely nodded, letting the words pass. Focusing, instead, on the unspoken affection he heard in the intern's voice. The same note that existed in Alison's when she'd first mentioned her brother.

Did he have a family? Was that kind of filial affection part of his life, too? He had no way of proving it right now, only the vaguest hint of a feeling, but he thought that he did. Or maybe it was just wishful thinking on his part.

Saying goodbye, Luc walked out of the hospital with Alison. He noticed that for once she wasn't talking very much. Probably trying to decide whether to drive him to the shelter, or let him walk there, he thought.

Alison held her tongue until they were outside in the parking lot again and alone. She unlocked the car doors, and then, unable to stand it any longer, her conscience pushed out the words.

"Look, I don't like the idea of your staying at one of these places."

"You don't," he repeated. He didn't know her. He had no way of knowing where she was going with this.

She looked at him, torn between guilt and the need to protect her privacy. Guilt won.

"No, I don't. I don't know if you saved my life or not, but you very well might have and I would be callous and ungrateful for the sacrifice your coming to my rescue apparently cost you if I let you stay at a flophouse overnight."

He took out the address the detective had given him and looked at it. "Flophouse?"

He was repeating things again. Alison didn't know how much clearer to make it for him. "Work with me here," she retorted.

The look on his face was innocent and compounded her guilt. "I would if I knew what we were working on."

Trying again, she enunciated each word. "I live at home. With my brothers. You just met Jimmy. There's Kevin, too. He's the oldest." Not that that mattered, she thought, except maybe to Kevin. But they each had a vote on what went on in the house. She knew she could count on Jimmy to back her up. "There's this room over the garage. It's not much, but it's clean and you wouldn't have to share your space with forty other people." And any assorted bugs and/or vermin that might decide to spend the night, as well, she added silently.

In his present state, with not even a glimmer of a memory to fall back on for guidance, Luc didn't want to presume too much. "Are you asking me to stay at your place?"

"No, I'm telling you you're staying at my place," she corrected tersely. "My garage," she amended. "That is—" Frustrated, she dragged a hand through her hair. "Look, I owe you, and I wouldn't feel very good about myself if I let you stay in one of these places."

The smile that came to his lips was slow in its progress, a little like sunrise when the sun reached up over the mountain range to clear a path for itself in the sky. She found herself staring at it. At him. And getting lost.

"Can't have you feeling bad about yourself," Luc agreed.

For the life of her, Alison couldn't tell if he was putting her on, teasing her or just being honest with her. In any case, she didn't have time to straighten it out right now. Glancing at her watch, she realized that she was overdue getting the cab back. Her shift had been over for ten minutes and she had nothing to show for it.

Except Luc.

She doubted that Kevin would think the afternoon had been very profitable.

He was out of his small, windowless office before she brought the cab to a full stop within the large garage where Kevin kept the five cabs that he owned. Slightly shorter and broader than his brother, Kevin Quintano gave the impression of a bulldozer plowing through the underbrush.

He was plowing in her direction now.

Having spent the better part of the last couple of hours trying to reach her on the two-way radio when she didn't arrive to pick up her next fare, Kevin had been vacillating between furious and frantic. She was, after all, his baby sister, and the city was large. All the maniacs were not confined to cities with more than a million in population.

Now that he saw she was all right, he went back to furious.

"Okay, what the hell's going on? I've been trying to reach you all afternoon. Where the hell did you disappear to? I felt like someone in that old sitcom. You know, *Car 54, Where Are You?* Except in this case—" he jerked a thumb in the cab's direction "—it was Cab 4." He waved one of his drivers over. "What are you waiting for? Christmas? Go, go!"

With a nod of his head, the driver eased past Alison and got in on the driver's side.

Hands on his hips, Kevin turned toward his sister. He didn't miss the opportunity to glare at the man with his sister, either. He knew it couldn't be a boyfriend. Gorgeous though she was, Alison didn't have boyfriends. He and the others had tried, in vain, to fix her up time and again, but she'd stubbornly refused to have any part of it.

When being yelled at, Alison had a tendency to yell back. It didn't affect the way she felt about her brother at all. "I didn't have time to call in."

"Why, why didn't you have time to call in?" Kevin found himself walking behind her as Alison retreated to his office, the stranger beside her. "Was it because of him? He get fresh with you?" Not waiting for an answer, Kevin moved Alison aside and commandeered the man's attention. "Listen, buddy, just because she was driving a cab doesn't make her an easy mark—"

Alison wedged herself between them, glaring at her brother. "Kevin, you're getting carried away again."

Deep-seated affection flickered in Kevin's eyes for a second as he looked at her. The ideas that had been running through his head these last few hours... "You're my baby sister. I have a right to get carried away if some guy—"

"He saved me, Kevin."

The barrage of words came to a sudden, skidding halt. Dark brows came together over a Roman nose. "Saved you? Saved you from what?"

"From being mugged." She'd wanted to find a way to tell him, a nice, calm way, but apparently Kevin wasn't going to allow that. "Two guys stole the fare money. And all his things. I'm sorry, Kevin. The money's gone."

He didn't give a damn about the money. Only Alison.

He looked from Luc to Alison, words temporarily refusing to come. And then they came. In a flood.

"That does it! No more driving the cab. Not full-time, not part-time. Not from here to the edge of the garage—"

"Kevin—"

But he wasn't listening. "I told you that wasn't a job for a woman, but no, you wouldn't listen. You always thought you knew what was best." When he thought of what could have happened to her, his blood ran cold. "Well, I've got news for you. You don't know—"

She placed her hand on her brother's shoulder. "Slow down, Kevin. Luc has a headache."

Working up a full head of steam, he was just getting started. "I don't care—"

But she did. "He got it defending me."

"Oh." The words finally penetrated. Chagrined, Kevin looked at the man who had earned his eternal gratitude. "Oh," he repeated. "Hey, sit down." He dragged a chair closer, urging Luc to sit. "You want an aspirin?" Kevin pulled open a drawer in his desk, reaching for a half-empty bottle. "Did you take him to see Jimmy—?"

Alison reclaimed the bottle and put it back in the drawer. "He has painkillers and yes, I took him to see Jimmy. I am a nurse, you know."

"A nurselet," Kevin corrected fondly. Ten years older than Alison, it was hard for him to think of her in any sort of adult capacity. "But you're coming along," he added when he saw the storm clouds gathering in her eyes.

Even though he had no way of knowing for sure, something told Luc that he was accustomed to a less frantic pace. But then, probably everyone was. "You people always talk this fast?"

Kevin looked at him and then laughed. He dragged his hand through his hair in a way that was reminiscent of Alison. "Only when we're stirred up," Kevin apologized. "Can I get you anything? Just name it."

"He needs a place to stay," Alison interjected before Luc could demur the offer. "If it's okay with you, I told him he could have the room over the garage. Until his memory comes back."

Kevin glanced in Luc's direction. "His memory?"

Alison nodded, pressing her lips together. "He has amnesia." And it was all her fault.

Kevin could only stare at her.

Chapter Three

"You can't remember anything?"

Kevin thought of all the things that were crowded into his life, all the treasured memories he had of precious moments. The idea of suddenly losing his grasp on all of them was devastating. Sympathy flooded through him for the young man sitting on the guest side of his small, cluttered desk.

"No." The single word echoed, dark and lonely, in Luc's brain. Drawing nothing into the light in its wake except frustration.

Blowing out a breath, Kevin passed his hand over his hair.

"Man, that has got to be awful for you." At a loss as to what to say, Kevin looked toward his sister. "How long do these kind of things last?"

Alison hesitated, then purposely kept her voice upbeat

for Luc's sake. "Jimmy said it might clear up in a day or two."

Or longer, she added silently. There was just no telling. Even though she'd asked the same question of Jimmy, Alison knew that there was no blueprint for amnesia to follow. It varied from person to person, a product of cause and effect. It could be gone by tomorrow, or last forever. There was just no telling.

For Luc's sake, she crossed her fingers and hoped for the first.

"Day or two, huh?" Kevin was a dyed-in-the-wool optimist. He shifted his eyes to look at Luc. "Sure he can stay over the garage," he told Alison. "You can stay for as long as it takes. Nothing's too good for the man who saved my little sister." As if to underscore his sentiment, Kevin threw an arm around Alison, hugging her to him.

Embarrassed, Alison tried not to flush. "We're a very close family," she told Luc.

Luc noticed that she subtly shrugged her brother's arm off and then stepped back. It reminded him of something. Small spaces and claustrophobia. Cave-ins. What did all that mean?

Behind him, he heard the door being opened. "Hey, Kevin, can I see you a sec?" Turning in his chair, he saw a man in stained, zipped-up coveralls peering into the office.

Kevin waved the mechanic back out. "In a minute, Matt. Can't you see I'm busy?"

Grunting, Matt retreated. "It'll keep."

An idea suddenly hit Kevin. Perching on the corner of his desk, he looked down at Luc. "Have you been to the police station?"

"No, but I called 911," Alison told him. "The police came to take down the information about the robbery."

"Yeah, that." He dismissed the robbery as unimportant. What mattered was that Alison wasn't hurt. Money was replaceable, she wasn't. "No, I mean about Luc here. They've got a Missing Persons Bureau, maybe they've got something like a Found Persons Bureau." It made perfect sense to him. There had to be more people wandering around with amnesia than just Luc.

Alison pressed her lips together, holding back a smile. She didn't want Kevin to think she was laughing at him. There were times when she envied her brother, the simplicity of his soul.

"He's only had amnesia for less than half a day. That means if he's 'missing,' he's only been so for that amount of time. If he's supposed to meet someone, they probably think he's just been delayed."

"Meeting someone." Kevin rolled the idea over in his head. There had to be possibilities they weren't seeing or tapping into. "Were you on your way to a meeting?"

"Well, he was on his way to a hotel," Alison told him. Told both of them, she realized. Luc was listening to her as intently as her brother was. She had to remind herself that this was news to him, as well. She wished he had talked more to her when he'd gotten into the cab. Some fares never stopped talking from the moment they got in until she brought them to their destination. But after the exchange of names, Luc had been fairly quiet.

"I picked him up at the airport."

The information felt like a depth charge aimed at a submarine. Kevin felt disappointment wash over him. "So you don't even live around here?"

Luc considered the question, turning it over in his

mind. Trying to find a bit of information that might begin to answer the query. But not even a glimmer pushed forward.

He sighed. "Not that I know of."

"There has to be something you remember." Kevin saw Alison opening her mouth, undoubtedly ready to launch into some sort of medical terminology. He was going with common sense. "People don't lose their total memory when they get amnesia. I mean, you still speak English and you know how to walk, right?" Eagerness built in his voice. "There's got to be something else rattling around in your head. You just don't know, you know."

There was that simplicity again, cutting to the heart of things. Alison looked at her brother with affection. "Sometimes, Kevin, I think you should have been a Rhodes scholar."

He had no time for compliments, though it was nice to be appreciated once in a while. "I know all the roads I need to, right here in Seattle." In his enthusiasm, Kevin leaned in closer to Luc. "Think. Is there anything? Anything at all?"

There was no harm in giving Kevin's theory a whirl, Alison thought. "Maybe if you closed your eyes, it might make you focus better."

Luc was game to try anything to jar at least a few thoughts loose. He did as she suggested. After a moment he opened his eyes again.

"Anything?" she pressed, eager. There was something there, she thought. In his eyes. He'd remembered something.

"Snow."

Alison stared at him, confused. "Excuse me?"

"I had an image of snow." But even as he said it, the

image was fading into oblivion. "Or maybe just a huge expanse of nothingness." *Brought on by wishful thinking,* he added silently. "I can't tell."

She placed a hand on his shoulder, leaving it there for a single beat before realizing what she was doing. Alison let her hand drop to her side. "It'll come to you. You're probably just trying too hard. Maybe after a good night's sleep—"

"It's only five o'clock in the afternoon," Kevin pointed out.

Maybe, but Luc had been through a lot and he was undoubtedly exhausted. Some of his color was returning, which was a good sign, but she didn't want to push it. Noticing his color, she realized that it looked as if he was tanned. Did he live on the coast? Near a beach? His way of speaking was relaxed, laid-back. Did that make him a Californian?

God, but she was lousy at playing detective. Where was Sherlock Holmes when you needed him?

"He can still get some rest, Kevin. C'mon, I'll take you home." Walking out of the office, she stopped abruptly. The space where she'd parked her car this morning was empty. She turned around to look at her brother. Kevin, she noticed, was walking slow, as if he expected the man beside him to collapse at any second. "Where's my car?"

"Oh." In all the excitement, he'd forgotten. "Matt parked it over by number 2. I had him do an oil change for you."

She'd purchased the secondhand car with money she'd earned doing odd jobs since she was sixteen years old. She treated the car as if it were a beloved pet. "I can do my own oil change."

"Yeah, I know." It was an old story. She always

balked whenever he tried to do something for her, acting as if he was impinging on her independence. She was that way with everyone. "But I enjoy doing little things for you." He glanced at Luc. "She likes to act feisty."

"No, just my age," she countered. And then she sighed, looking at Luc. She'd been over this ground before, more times than she could count. "Being the youngest, they all think they have to take care of me."

"We do," Kevin confided to Luc, winking broadly for Alison's benefit. "You know how it is."

"No," Luc replied, a wave of regret washing over him. "I don't."

"Yeah, right. Sorry." Embarrassed at his blunder, Kevin looked away. He dug into his pocket, extracting his wallet and handed two twenties to Luc. "You gotta be hungry. Get yourself something to eat—on me."

Alison gave up. There was no point in saying that she was perfectly capable of paying for both of them. Who was Kevin going to baby once she was gone? She'd put in her application to several medically depressed areas in the country and gotten back favorable responses. At this point she was just trying to decide which to accept. Kevin was going to have a lot of adjusting to do.

But for now she humored him. "We'll pick up something on the way."

Maybe you can pick up a wife on the way.

Almost in a trance, Luc stopped walking. "A wife."

Alison and Kevin turned in unison to look at Luc, both stunned.

Maybe she'd heard wrong. "What?"

Luc looked at them, just as surprised as they were by what had just come out of his mouth. Very carefully he examined the words that had flashed through his head. But even now they were fading away.

"Someone said that to me...I think. Something about...looking for a wife, picking up a wife on the way. Something like that." It made less and less sense the more he said it.

Alison laughed shortly. "I didn't know they were holding a wife special at the mall." At best, it was an odd clue to the man's identity. Did he mean picking up *his* wife, she wondered. Could that be it? He was married and meeting his wife?

Luc tried to hear a voice, attach a face to the speaker, but it was like dropping cotton candy into the water. The words, the memory was dissolving before he could reach it.

"It had something to do with my coming here. Or maybe not," he added with a helpless shrug of his shoulders. None of it was getting any clearer. If anything, it was becoming murkier.

For all he knew, the line that had echoed in his mind might have been something he'd heard in a movie or a television program.

He looked as if he was getting exasperated. She couldn't blame him. Wanting to distract Luc, she said, "Let's go get you settled in."

To Kevin, it seemed like an odd way to put it. "What's there to settle? The man has nothing but the clothes on his back."

Kevin was right. Luc was going to need something else to wear. She scrutinized Luc closely. "Jimmy's about the same size," she judged.

"Better check with Jimmy first," Kevin cautioned. In all likelihood, Jimmy would be generous, but you never knew. "You know how he is about his clothes."

She laughed, remembering the one time she'd needed a tailored shirt and had to pilfer it out of Jimmy's closet.

The tirade when he discovered the loss had been unbelievable. Especially after he'd seen the wine stains. "Beau Brummell was probably more willing to give his clothes away."

"Beau Brummell. Nineteenth-century figure, known for his penchant for finery. Friend of the prince of Wales."

She and Kevin exchanged looks, then turned to look at Luc, who appeared a little amazed himself. He had no idea where that had come from.

"Maybe you're an encyclopedia salesman," Kevin suggested, only half kidding.

Luc shrugged. "Right now, that sounds as right as anything."

Like a child on his first trip away from home, he watched the scenery go by outside the car window. Trying to absorb everything. Feeling a little lost, a little uncertain.

Except in his case, Luc hadn't a clue where home actually was. All he knew, and not even with any amount of certainty, was that it wasn't here.

"You're trying too hard."

Her voice, soft, understanding, drew his attention back to the car he was in. And to her. "What?"

She'd noted his reflection in the window when they'd stopped at the last traffic light. Alison could have sworn she could see his eyes getting tread worn. Though she'd never experienced anything remotely like amnesia, she could well imagine how frustrating it had to be for him. To think and not remember. To exist and have absolutely no memory of it.

"You're trying too hard. To remember," she added

after a moment. "Sometimes, things come when you least expect them."

Luc turned around to face her. Something she'd said was nudging a piece of a thought in his mind. Setting it off.

But it was shimmering just out of reach, just out of focus. For all he knew, it could be animal, vegetable or mineral. For the time being, he left it alone. Not that he had much choice in the matter.

"Yeah, maybe you're right." Maybe if he allowed his mind to remain a blank, the pieces would eventually turn up.

He saw her grin and felt something stir inside him in response. The grin was sensual, but innocent at the same time. More questions came to mind, but this time they had to do with her.

"I usually am." And then Alison laughed. "Not that anyone in my family likes to admit it."

Family. The word created ripples of a feeling that passed over him. Again it defied capture. He couldn't quite make it his. Maybe if he kept her talking, the feeling would crystallize into something he could identify.

"How many are there in your family?"

"Four, counting me." It had been four for a very long time. Her mother had died when she was eight, her father three years after that. For all intents and purposes, Kevin was as much her parent as he was her brother. "You met Kevin and Jimmy. Among the missing, but only for the moment, is Lily." She grinned again. They were as different as night and day, she and her sister. Lily was the sophisticate. "Lily recently moved out to live over the restaurant she bought into."

Lily had finally managed to buy out the other owners and rechristen the restaurant. There was no doubt in her mind that within the year, Lily's would become the trendy place to go in Seattle. Lily wouldn't have it any other way.

Alison glanced at Luc as she took a side street. It wasn't far now. "In case you haven't noticed, we're all eager little beavers in my family."

"I noticed." Except that he would have used the word *enterprising,* he thought, then wondered where the word had come from. "And you're the youngest."

She laughed and nodded. At times, it was more of a condition than a chronological position. "And they never let me forget it." She hesitated, then decided to prod a little. Who knew? It might actually help. "Do you think you have any family?"

He'd been asking himself the same thing. With no results. "I don't know, but I don't think so, at least not in the traditional way." He tried to make sense of it for himself as well as her. "There's this vague feeling that there's someone, but…not really."

That didn't make a hell of a whole lot of sense, did it, he thought. And yet he couldn't shake the feeling that there had been someone, someone important, who wasn't there anymore. Had they died? A hollow feeling took hold of him as the realization sank in. Someone important to him could have died recently and he didn't even know.

Without thinking, she slipped her hand over his in mute comfort, then replaced it on the steering wheel. "Sounds like a ghost."

"That," he agreed. "Or something that wasn't." The words drifted from his lips slowly, just as the thought had drifted in. It wasn't the death of a person that he was feeling, but of something. What did that mean?

"I don't follow you."

That made two of them, he thought ruefully. "Sorry, it's just something that seemed to pop into my head and then out again." And he couldn't make a damn bit of sense out of it.

She didn't want him getting too frustrated, not when she thought he was still weak.

"Well, when it pops back in, try to hang on to it. Something tells me those missing pieces of your puzzle are doing their damnedest to try to show up again." Pulling up to a compact, two-story house, she parked at the curb. They took turns using the garage. This week, Kevin's car and Jimmy's motorcycle got to stay out of Seattle's daily mist. "In the meantime, this is where you can crash."

"Crash?"

She shut off the engine and got out. "Set up your tent." Walking ahead of him, she led the way to the detached garage. There was a wooden staircase on the side closer to the house. "Park your body. You know, stay."

For the first time since he'd opened his eyes, amusement materialized. "Do you always use this many words?"

She took the wooden stairs two at a time. "I love the sound of words." Reaching the landing, she unlocked the door. She turned around and waited for him to join her. "I was going to become an English teacher, but then I thought that wouldn't make enough of a difference." She let him walk in first.

The room was small, made smaller by the presence of a queen-size bed and a massive chest of drawers that had once occupied the master bedroom. "Does that mean a lot to you, making a difference?"

There was no way she could put into words just how

much it did mean. No one really knew or understood. Sometimes, the feeling even left her a little mystified.

"When you're the littlest and the youngest, you have a tendency to want to be the loudest just to be noticed. I want to make a difference, to know that because of me, someone feels better. *Is* better." That's why nursing had seemed so right to her. It allowed her the time to hold a patient's hand, to offer comfort. In order to heal, the spirit had to be helped along as well as the body. Hearing herself, Alison stopped abruptly. "I'm talking too much."

He didn't want her to stop. "No, please, talk. Listening to you helps fill up the empty spaces in my head."

For some reason, there wasn't enough air in the room. She'd never noticed how small the room was. How tight the space around the bed seemed. There was no place to back up and suddenly she felt as if she needed to.

"You should be filling them up with your own thoughts."

He smiled at the irony of her words. "I seem to have misplaced them. Temporarily I hope."

"Do you think you're married?" She had no idea where the question came from. Or why she wanted to know. Her curiosity didn't feel idle, but active. It made her uneasy. Trying to move around Luc, Alison maneuvered toward the door and opened it.

"I don't know." He searched, recalled nothing. "What does being married feel like?"

It took effort not to shiver as she remembered her own short, disastrous venture. Buried two years in her past, the mark it had left behind was still vivid. "Like you can't breathe."

"Then I'm not married."

He probably thought she was strange, if not crazy.

Needing something to do, she crossed to the window, opening it. The room hadn't been aired out since their cousin had come to spend the holidays with them last Christmas. "Sorry, that was harsh. I shouldn't have said that."

She needed to be moving all the time. Was that because she had so much energy to spare, or was she trying to outdistance something? There'd been a note in her voice he couldn't quite recognize. Not that, he thought, he'd recognize a hell of a whole lot right now.

"Why not?"

"Because I just shouldn't have." Why couldn't he leave it at that? It was his mind they needed to explore, not hers. "Besides, you're a stranger."

"And your husband wouldn't like you talking to strangers," he guessed.

"I'm not married." He probably didn't make the connection, or remember at any rate. "I live here, remember?"

Luc watched her fuss with the bedspread. "Yes, it's just that I thought maybe you lived here with your husband. You sounded so adamant just now, about marriage."

She had, too. Probably too adamant. Alison ran her hand along her neck, trying to lighten the moment. "It's been a rough day. I was almost mugged."

His eyes met hers. Humor glinted in them. "Yeah, I know."

It felt as if his eyes were touching her. Air became thick in her throat, almost solidifying. She turned away, unsettled by the pull she felt. "There's a tiny bathroom in the back. No shower, but you can wash your hands. I know it's not much, but—"

"I don't need much," he assured her. There was no

need to apologize. She and her brother were being more than kind, taking in a stranger. "And I appreciate you and your brothers letting me stay here."

The image of a small room, dark but warm, flashed through his brain, remaining in less time than it took to identify it.

Alison touched his arm, drawing his attention back into the room above the garage. "What is it?"

He blinked, trying to focus. Aware only of the fact that she was standing very close to him again. And that she wore a fragrance that reminded him of—what? "Hmm?"

"You just had a very strange look on your face. Did you just remember something?"

"A half of something," he allowed. "A room." He turned around slowly, taking in the details of the room for the first time. The room in his mind had been cheerier. "Kind of like this. It was dark. Outside," he realized, "it was dark."

"Nighttime," she guessed.

He was about to agree, then stopped. "No, it wasn't. It was daytime."

Then why was it dark? "A storm?" Or maybe his mind was playing tricks on him.

It sounded like a logical guess, but he couldn't really say for sure. "I don't know."

Her heart went out to him. In his place, she wouldn't have known if she could stand it as calmly as he was. "I'm sorry, I shouldn't be plying you with questions. It's just that I keep thinking if I ask the right one, suddenly everything'll come back to you."

He smiled, grateful for her help. She made him feel less alone. "It beats you hitting me on the head, hoping that might jar the thoughts back into my brain."

She'd seen a cartoon like that once. Maybe, subconsciously, he was remembering the same one. "If everything else fails, maybe we'll fall back on that." She remembered Kevin giving Luc money for dinner. She'd forgotten to stop at the store. "Why don't you follow me into the house and we can see what there is in the refrigerator to heat up?" If she was lucky, Lily had stopped by to stock it for them.

"Sounds like a plan, and since I don't seem to have any previous engagements that I'm aware of, I happen to be free." He opened the door and waited for her to step through.

Something sizzled in her veins as she did so. Surprised, she suppressed it.

Chapter Four

The kitchen was state-of-the-art, with highly polished, copper pots and pans hanging from ceiling hooks arranged in a rectangle that encompassed the fluorescent light fixture. A butcher-block island stood in the middle, unadorned and vacant, while a blue-tiled utility bar housed only newspapers from days past and a small television set that was dormant at the moment.

It was a kitchen waiting in vain to be pressed into service.

This had been Lily's domain. For a time, Alison had felt intimidated and inadequate just walking into it until she'd made her peace with the fact that she enjoyed eating sandwiches and two-minute microwave specials.

Leading the way in, she opened both sides of the refrigerator, allowing Luc a full view of the interior. It was Jimmy's turn to go shopping. Which would explain why there was so little within the "magic box," as she used to call it when she was a little girl. Back then, her mother had presided here and she could remember warm, wonderful smells coupled with a feeling of well-being coming from this room. There'd been no pots hanging from the ceiling, no butcher-block island then, only a breakfast nook. And love.

Until everything had changed.

"Okay." She glanced over her shoulder at Luc. "What's your pleasure?"

The question caught him unprepared. He'd just allowed his mind to wander, to dwell on the woman who had taken him under her wing because, according to her, he'd come to her rescue. He wished he could remember at least that part. But he couldn't.

Instead, what was teasing his mind now was the very real, very strong attraction he was experiencing standing so close to her. *Pleasure* was the word for it, all right.

"Excuse me?"

"Food." She gestured toward the open freezer. Stacked inside were several colorful boxes, the names on the side hinting at culinary heaven in under five minutes. She tilted her head so that she could read the labels better. Her hair brushed along his bare arm, sending ripples of current through him. "We have frozen pot pie, frozen Mexican entrée, frozen—" Straightening, she looked at him with a self-depreciating smile. "Well, pretty much frozen everything."

He was more interested in the other side of the refrigerator. Edging her to the side, he indicated the contents on the lower two shelves. "You've got some vegetables and a carton of eggs."

There was no point in even mentioning that. "I don't want to add ptomaine poisoning to your list of troubles." She began to close that side of the refrigerator.

He placed his hand in the way, stopping her. "Why, are they spoiled?" Reaching inside, he picked up the larger of the two red peppers languishing beside the three sprigs of broccoli and pressed his fingers along the sides. "Feels pretty firm to me."

She had no idea why she was identifying with an inanimate object. Why she could almost feel his fingertips pressing her skin. Maybe, she decided, because Luc wasn't quite real. Without a memory, he could be anyone, like a fantasy come to life for a brief spate of time. Once his memory returned, he'd be gone.

And she would remain unthreatened.

"They're not spoiled—" she agreed. "Yet. But they would be by the time I get through with whatever I tried to make." A person had to know her limitations. This was one of hers. "We have a division of labor here as far as the kitchen goes," she explained, taking the pepper from him and returning it to its place. "Whenever she stops by, Lily creates, Kevin cooks, Jimmy warms up and I destroy." She made it a point to stay out of the kitchen, except to eat, whenever humanly possible.

He couldn't quite wrap his mind around what she was saying. "You can't be as bad as all that."

"I wouldn't place any bets on that if I were you." She glanced overhead at the pan hanging closest to her. "I stand a better chance winning a tennis match with a frying pan than I do making an edible meal with it."

He hardly heard her answer. Something had just come to him. Too vague to be labeled a memory, it was almost like a feeling. "I've had too much frozen."

Instantly alert, she grasped at the information, wanting to coax more out. "You remember eating frozen food?"

"No." That wasn't it. He strained, trying to catch hold of the silvery thread, to expand it into something larger. Something tangible he could handle. "I remember—ice, lots of it." His eyes seemed to glow with the fragmented thought. "And snow."

It was progress. Of a sort, she supposed. But such vague progress, it was hard not to sound discouraged. "That could be anywhere except for Southern California and Hawaii. What else do you remember?"

There was a blank. A huge blank. Hoping to stimulate something more, Luc stared into the open vegetable crisper again.

"I'm not sure." And then he saw a stove in his mind's eye. A large, six-burner, industrial gas stove. He could almost feel the heat. His eyes widened as he turned toward her. "Cooking, I remember—cooking."

His smile was wide and boyishly engaging. Alison could almost feel it burrowing into her. Seeking a response. Her heart fluttered. But that was only in empathy. She was identifying with him at this breakthrough he was having. There couldn't be any other reason for it.

Derek had taught her that she wasn't meant for things like romance and love. *If you can't swim, don't put your toe into the water.*

She kept her toes where they belonged.

But she couldn't help the wave of enthusiasm she felt for Luc. "See, it's coming back to you already. You want to fool around in the kitchen?" He looked at her, bemused. Or maybe amused. She realized what that had to have sounded like. "With the ingredients I mean." Moving quickly, wanting to cover the flustered feeling that had suddenly hit her from left field, she took out the peppers and lined them up on the counter. "Maybe something'll come back to you."

Something already had. A wave of bittersweetness. A

sense of loss and resignation, sneaking up out of nowhere and drenching him. But loss of what? Resignation over what?

About what?

Or who?

All questions echoing in his brain, having no answers.

"You're trying too hard again." She smoothed back the furrow between his eyes even as he shifted them toward her questioningly. Realizing that maybe she was stepping over some invisible line that was best kept enforced, she dropped her hand to her side. "The last flash came to you without any effort on your part. The rest will, too. Maybe even by morning." At least, it certainly looked promising enough. She peered at him. He no longer looked as if he was staving off agony. "How's your headache, by the way?"

He'd forgotten about it until she'd mentioned it just now. "Almost gone." The realization surprised him as much as it pleased him.

Another good sign. Jimmy had given him an injection to mute the pain, but that had been a while ago and she knew he hadn't taken any of the pills that her brother had given him. There was every indication that their houseguest wouldn't be staying long.

And that, of course, was for the good, she told herself.

"Then maybe puttering around in the kitchen might not be a bad idea." She was already taking out the carton and placing it on the counter beside the peppers. If he needed anything more, he was going to have to tell her. "See what you can cook up—for you and for me."

He said the first thing that suggested itself. "An omelet?"

He said it as if he thought it was the wrong time of

day for it. She'd been raised on eggs at night and steak in the morning. Food was food.

"Hey, I'm hungry enough to eat waxed paper. An omelet sounds like heaven." She paused, not knowing what he needed in addition to the two ingredients she'd put out. "I'd offer to help cook, but that's a contradiction in terms as far as I'm concerned." And then she grinned. "I can be your cheering section."

His cheering section. She'd put into words just how he saw her. "I'd like that."

She closed her eyes, savoring this bite as much as she had the first and the second. The man was nothing short of a miracle worker. He even cooked rings around Lily. This wasn't an omelet, it was a minor miracle.

Lily was going to love him.

As if her older sister needed another man in her life. The thought was without malice. Dedicated, hardworking, Lily also knew how to play hard. And to enjoy herself.

Not for you, Alison. You were meant for other things, she told herself.

She held up her empty fork, raising a phantom glass in a toast.

"Where did you learn to cook like that?" And then her question hit her. If he could answer that, then he wouldn't have been here in the first place. She offered him an apologetic look. "Sorry, I was just trying to sneak out another piece of information."

It was an excuse, a way of covering for herself. But now that she said it, she realized that it wasn't such a bad way to go. If she talked enough, prodded enough, maybe something else would come back to him. Maybe even everything.

"The subconscious is a strange thing." She fell back on textbook knowledge. He was, after all, her first amnesia patient. And he was her responsibility, as well, because she meant to have him get better in her care. "It's all in there, you know, every thought you've ever had, every memory you ever gathered." Her eyes strayed to the small TV set on the counter near the sink. It was there at her insistence. "And every program you ever watched."

He followed her line of vision and reflected. "I don't think I've watched many programs."

The concept, voluntarily adhered to, was almost impossible for her to believe. Unless there was a reason. Her eyes lit up. Worth a shot.

"Maybe your parents were disciplinarians. I had a friend whose parents would only let her watch one hour of television a week. Me, I was plugged into a television set the day I was born. Kevin says I'm a walking trivia book on cartoons and sitcoms."

She stopped to take in another forkful. Every one had been a delight. "This is really great. You know, if this amnesia of yours continues for a while and you need a job, I know Lily would love to get her hands on you."

Probably literally and otherwise, she added silently. Lily had radar as far as good-looking men went. Luc not only fell into the category, he looked as if he could probably rise to the head of the column.

"Right now, she can't find a chef to meet her standards, so she's doing all the cooking at Lily's herself." She finished her meal and felt a pang of regret. She was full, but she would have been willing to eat more. A lot more. "If you can make anything else besides omelets, you'd be an answer to a prayer for her."

"I can cook anything." He grinned at the cocky way

that sounded. But there was no denying the wave of confidence that had come over him. He *knew* he could cook. It was nice to finally be sure of something, even something as trivial as this. "I can."

Using her fork as a microphone, she pretended to be a news announcer and declared, "And we've established a beachhead." Her eyes were eager. "Anything else coming back to you?"

"You already asked that."

"I thought we'd do spot checks every hour, see if anything else drifts back to you." She propped her head up on her fisted hand. "Like, do you remember saving anyone else?"

He wondered if she knew how genial her smile was. How warm. He shook his head in answer to her question. "I don't even remember saving you."

"You did. You were like the U.S. cavalry. Or a Canadian Mountie." They were near the Canadian border. Maybe he was a Canadian, on vacation in the States. If that were the case, this would probably go down as one of the worst vacations on record, just a few lines below booking passage on the *Titanic*.

She could tell he wanted her to elaborate. "You hauled that guy out of the cab as if he was some rag doll instead of this stocky pig." Alison smiled, recalling. "He looked really scared, even though he had a knife and you just had your bare hands."

None of this was coming back to him. It was as if she was talking about something that had happened to someone else. "Did I hit him?"

She laughed. "Into next Sunday. If he hadn't had a partner skulking in the shadows, he would have been cooling his heels in jail right now." Her narrative over, her voice softened. "And you would still have your memory. I'm really very sorry about that."

He didn't want her feeling guilty. "It's not your fault."

But she didn't see it that way. "I should have parked in the street." One little misstep had caused all this. "It was just that I wanted to avoid getting snarled up in traffic."

He dismissed it with a shrug, wanting her to do the same. Leaning over, he picked up her empty plate as well as his own and rose to his feet. "Logical."

A smile curved her lips as she watched him. "You do dishes, too?"

He looked down at the plates and realized that he was bringing them over to the sink. He'd done it automatically, as if he'd been preprogrammed. "I guess I do."

The man was single. If she hadn't decided the matter earlier, this would have convinced her. "Well, memory loss or not, you're not going to be on the market long." Getting up, she pushed in her chair. "You cook, clean up after yourself and put yourself on the line to rescue damsels in distress. Most women go to bed every night praying to meet someone like you."

Lowering the dishes into the sink, he turned to look at her. His eyes met hers. "Do you?"

Walked right into that one, didn't you? The look in his eyes had her backpedaling. "I'm not most women." Cleaning away the napkins, she purposely avoided his eyes. "Besides, I'm too busy."

"Doing what, besides driving the cab?" He wanted to know about her. To find out everything he could to satisfy this thirst to know things.

"That's only part-time and to help Kevin out if one of his regulars calls in sick. Like today." Taking a sponge, she wiped down the table. "Until a couple of weeks ago, I was a nursing student."

He opened the cabinet and looked for the dishwashing liquid. "What happened a couple of weeks ago?"

Moving around him, she opened the cabinet just under the sink and retrieved the bottle. She offered it to him. "I graduated." There was that look in his eyes again, like a piece of the puzzle was flying in front of him and he was trying to catch hold of it. "What? Did you just graduate, too?"

"No." The word *school* didn't conjure up any mental images for him. It was another one that had caught his attention. "Nursing..." He couldn't pull any of it together, but there was this feeling that someone had mentioned something about nursing, or nurses to him recently.

"You're a nurse?" When he made no response, Alison tried again, shooting another question at him. Hoping to nudge something loose in his mind. It was a little, she mused, like trying to get a computer to unfreeze, or at least re-boot. "You want a nurse," she guessed.

"No." But he didn't mean that, he realized. Looking at her, he could feel something pulling inside him. Something stirring. He couldn't begin to identify what, or why. But the word *want* had something to do with it. "That is, not exactly."

He'd been the one to receive the blow to the head, so why was she feeling weak in the knees? "Um, maybe I'd better wash and you sit down. This has to have been a strain for you, cooking and all." She all but pushed him toward the chair again. "And you've been on your feet too much."

"I ate sitting down," he pointed out.

Well, whatever else was wrong, his stubborn streak was alive and well. She moved the chair closer to him.

"Humor me, I'm the professional here." And then she stopped, realizing that she couldn't actually make that assumption. "At least, I think I'm the only professional here."

Luc ignored the chair. "Meaning what?"

"Meaning you could be anything." She looked at him, trying to picture the kind of career he might have gravitated toward. All she had to go on was basic instinct rather than any real input. She decided to let her imagination run wild. "A doctor, a vacationing postal employee, a billionaire in disguise, a disgruntled CIA assassin trying to catch a little R&R." She laughed at the absurdity of the last suggestion as the words died away.

The sound went right through him, a ray of sunshine in the midst of gloom. He felt himself smiling. "I guess that means you probably think we should rule out the last choice."

She hadn't meant to make it sound as if she were laughing at him. "I'm sorry, you just don't look like the hit-man type. Too clean, even though…"

She pressed her lips together. When was she ever going to learn to think things through before she started saying them out loud?

"Even though what?" he prodded, curious. Every word could be a clue, hopefully leading him that much more quickly back to familiar ground.

Well, she started it, she thought, she might as well finish it. The last thing he needed was for her to turn enigmatic on him. "Even though there's that sexy edge to you."

"Sexy?" What sort of feelings went along with being sexy? "You think I have a sexy edge?"

"Just being impartially observant." She turned away, feeling as if she'd stuck her foot in her mouth up to her ankle. Changing the subject, she opened the refrigerator again. "Want something to drink? You didn't have anything with your meal."

Drinks are on me.

Hey, Luc, we need more beer over here.

"Bartender."

Can of cola in her hand, she'd just popped the top and began to offer it to him. "You want something alcoholic to drink?" She could feel her stomach tightening. *Stop it,* she ordered. "I think there might be a six-pack in a cooler in the garage. I can check."

"No, don't." He caught her by the shoulder before she could go. "I don't want a beer."

"Okay," she allowed slowly, her eyes on his. She was desperately trying to follow him and not add to the confusion he had to be feeling. "But you did say 'bartender.' Are you remembering something? A bartender?" Someone from his past? "Or are you a bartender?"

Formless thoughts collided in his mind, refusing to come together. He combed his hand through his hair. The headache was whispering along his temples again.

"I don't know. I should, but I don't. Maybe I am. Or was."

There were other possibilities. "Or walked into a bar at the airport just before you caught your flight." Walked in, maybe, but didn't stay to have a drink, she thought. "You didn't have alcohol on your breath when I picked you up."

"You could smell my breath?"

"Not exactly, but when I picked you up, the windows in the cab were all closed. I was running the air conditioner. If you'd been drinking, I would have been able to pick up the scent in a couple of minutes. I once had this salesman in the cab, fresh from some convention. The whole cab seemed to fill up by the time we reached his destination.'' She didn't add that she'd driven almost the entire way with a churning stomach, even though she'd opened the front window over the passenger's protest. It had been raining heavily at the time. ''Matt had to practically fumigate the thing before I took the cab out again.'' The look on his face told her that he didn't quite understand why the taxi mechanic would have to do that. ''The smell of alcohol makes me gag.''

Okay, maybe he didn't know his last name, but some things, as Kevin had pointed out, did seem to stick with him. ''Isn't that kind of a strange allergy?''

''Unusual, maybe,'' she allowed, her tone dismissing any follow-up to the question.

It wasn't an allergy for her so much as it stirred up a memory. A recollection she wanted to be free of, but that continued to haunt her nonetheless, thirteen years later. The pungent smell of whiskey swirling around her, assaulting her mouth even as Jack tightened his fingers around her wrist...

''What's the matter?''

She realized that he was looking at her closely. Alison straightened. ''What?''

The color had drained from her face suddenly, as if she'd remembered something that bothered her. ''You look pale.''

She laughed it off. ''I haven't been getting enough sleep lately.'' And then she looked at him, one eyebrow raised. ''And besides, who's the nurse here?''

''You.'' And then he added with a smile, ''As far as we know.''

She thought that one over. It didn't fit. "I don't think so. I can't picture you as a nurse any more than I can as a hit man."

He crossed his arms before him gamely. "Okay, what do you picture me as?"

That took her a moment. She scrutinized him slowly, taking in each feature. His face was just the slightest bit chiseled, at odds with the boyish impression he first cast. And there was nothing boyish about his shoulders or the muscles in his forearms. That was all man. As was the way he moved and stood, with his weight evenly distributed while balancing on the balls of his feet. A tiger ready to spring into action—just the way he had in the alley.

"A cowboy?" she finally ventured. He probably wasn't, but he certainly looked like every woman's fantasy of a cowboy. His skin was even a golden tan, unless he came by the coloring naturally via an enviable gene pool.

No bells rang, but the idea amused him. He grinned. "Do I have my own ranch, or do I work for someone?"

Enjoying herself, a little lost in the way he smiled, she played along. "Both. You started out working for someone, maybe your father, and then saved up enough to get your own place."

He nodded, his expression thoughtful. "Horses or cattle?"

Carrying the fantasy a little further, she could see him in the saddle, his knees in tight against his mount's flanks, hands occupied with a lariat. An untamed colt trying to escape. And failing.

"You're more the horse type." And then she gave up the game, laughing at the scenario she'd just verbally sketched. "You're probably some computer wizard."

Even as she said it, the idea gained breadth and appeal. Computers were the burgeoning field. Dropping the dish towel she was holding on the table, she took his hand, eager to see if she was right. She crossed to the rear of the house.

"C'mon, why don't we find out?"

He knew his mind was fuzzy and that's why he wasn't following her, but he couldn't help wondering if his mind had ever been able to jump around the way hers did. "If I'm a wizard?"

"Well, maybe not a wizard, but if you know anything about computers at any rate."

Opening the door, she took him into the den. Books and papers were strewn on every available surface. Many had found their way to the rug either by design, or accident. Kevin did his bookkeeping here, and she and Jimmy put in their hours studying here. It looked like a paper war zone.

Stepping over a sliding mound of books, she reached the desk. An apologetic grin flashed at him over her shoulder. "Sorry about the mess, but we all share Big Al."

"Big Al?"

"The computer." There was affection in her voice, as if she was talking about a person rather than a collection of slotted cards, semiconductors and massive wires tangled in hopeless knots. She patted the oversize monitor. "I named it."

He looked for some indication as to why that and not something else. Like a company logo or an acronym. But there was nothing. He'd bite. "Why Big Al?"

She shrugged. "It seemed to fit." Reaching around the side of the minitower, she switched the computer on.

Humming began instantly. Within seconds, it was up and running.

Taking the pile of papers off the chair, she set them on the floor. "Okay, sit down."

But he didn't. Instead, he looked at the icons on the screen. They neither looked familiar, nor strange. They were just there. "And then do what?"

"Whatever comes naturally."

Luc paused for a moment, thinking. Trying to connect what he was feeling with a tangible action.

"Okay."

But instead of sitting down at the computer, he took a very stunned Alison into his arms and kissed her.

Chapter Five

*W*izard.

A first-class wizard.

The thought vibrated through Alison's brain. If there were such things as wizards, and they could indeed cast spells over unsuspecting mortals, then this man was certainly one of them.

Because, for one brief moment, Luc had cast a spell over her. That had to be it. Otherwise, why else was she still here, lost in this uncharted region and wanting to embrace it instead of pushing him angrily away, demanding to know what the hell he thought he was doing?

He knew damn well what he was doing.

But she didn't.

Not exactly. And her reaction to it was tearing her in half because part of her wanted to run while the other part wanted to linger. To savor.

The protest that sprang to her lips on contact died the

same moment. Disappearing as if it had never been. Instead of the suffocating fear and driving fury that had always lurked in the shadows whenever Derek had tried to make love to her, something else was going on.

Something else was happening within her.

It was almost as frightening as her reaction to anyone's touch. But at the same time, it was a different kind of frightening. It was softer, a great deal softer. And incredibly seductive. She couldn't begin to explain it.

There was a different fear now than what she'd experienced before. Fear of the unknown rather than fear of the known. Because to Alison, Luc represented the unknown.

He tasted of something dark and exciting, rather than of beer and demanding appetites. There was a gentleness to him that she found captivating. Soothing even while it was arousing. His lips moved over hers slowly, coaxing, drawing her out.

Her pulse raced, rushing toward some unknown goal line that was never to be reached. But she couldn't stop the racing, even though she tried.

She held her body rigid, stiff. But even as she did so, the stiffness was easing away.

Luc had had no idea, until he was smack-dab in the middle of it, that he was going to kiss her. He wasn't even sure what had come over him. It was just that, when Alison had told him to do what came naturally, this was all that occurred to him: an overwhelming, sudden desire to kiss her.

He had no recollection of kissing another woman, no recollection of ever wanting to. So for him, at least at this junction, this was something brand-new.

And it packed a wallop that nearly knocked him on

his butt, igniting other desires rather than satisfying the one he'd had.

The degree with which he wanted her took him by storm and stunned him.

It took effort to draw back, to surrender what he'd laid claim to. Her expression when he drew his head away was impassive, but there was something in her eyes. Fear. Guilt kicked him in the ribs, stealing his breath almost as effectively as she had done only a moment ago.

She'd said he'd come to her aid and now here he was, frightening her. He wasn't sure just what had come over him.

"I'm sorry, that's no way to pay you back for your hospitality." He wanted to touch her, to comfort her, but knew that would only make things worse. Helpless, he shoved his hands into his pockets and wished himself somewhere else.

The words, kind, apologetic, were incongruous with the sentiment raised by the kiss that had just passed between them. More than that, they were almost on opposite ends of the spectrum he'd just opened up for her. She didn't know what to make of him.

Trying to be blasé, Alison shrugged. "Oh, I don't know. In some books it would have been."

He had no gift of gab to fall back on, no charm like…like who? There was someone in his life who could have talked his way out of this, but it wasn't him, and for now that was all that mattered. Later, maybe it would come to him.

Luc went with honesty. It was his only weapon. He hoped it was enough. "I just suddenly wanted to kiss you. So I did."

Yes, he certainly did. Alison knew that if she'd been

anyone else…but she wasn't. She had a history and she couldn't escape it or deny it, no matter how desperately she wanted to at times. It haunted her like a smudge made by a laundry marker, a smudge that couldn't be washed away.

She caught her lower lip between her teeth, hating the fact that she felt nervous. ''Any more sudden urges I should know about?''

That look he'd seen in her eyes still bothered him, but he knew any reference to it would only be met with her terse denial—and they'd both feel even more awkward than they did right at this moment. ''No, I think I can keep things under control.''

She wished he'd kept his lips under control, as well. She didn't like this feeling that was pervading her. Nerves skittered through her like tiny mice running for high ground, away from waters that were rising dangerously.

The best way to proceed, she decided, was to pretend that she hadn't been affected. And that she hadn't come dangerously close to being unraveled.

Alison indicated the computer. ''Do you want to see if you're as familiar with a computer as you are with raising pulses?''

Straddling the chair next to the computer, he looked up at her. A grin played along his lips. ''Then you felt something, too?''

Maybe honesty was the best way to go after all. He was making it sound as if he'd been just as stunned by the kiss as she was. No suggestions of continuing, no chest beating like some male gorilla, positive that every woman wanted him.

She felt a small smile tugging on her lips. ''I would have had to have been a stone not to.'' She pulled over another chair to the desk, moving aside a pile of papers. "I can't believe you're walking around free."

He looked down at the mouse pad. It showed an arctic scene. For a fleeing instant he was transported. "There aren't many women around." Even as the words came, he had no idea what prompted him to say them.

Alison looked at him. "Sure there are." And then she stopped. It was as if part of him wasn't in the room. Part of him was struggling to grasp another fragment. Compassion nudged out unease. "Did you just remember something?"

Luc blew out a breath, temporarily surrendering. "I thought I did, but it's gone now."

Luc saw a glimmer of his reflection on the monitor. At this angle, he looked ghostly, just like his thoughts. He kept feeling these surges through his brain, flashes of images, words telegraphing themselves across his mind. It was exhausting. Worse, because he had nothing to show for it. No larger pieces to put together, no memories suddenly returning.

"It's a little like being in a storm that's knocked the power lines out," he speculated. "Electricity keeps trying to come through, making fitful starts and stops and a lot of crackling noises, but the room doesn't get lit. I can't make out any of the shapes—they're still in the dark." *Just like I am.*

He seemed to know what he was talking about. She tried to build on his imagery. "Maybe it's stormy where you come from."

"Maybe," he allowed. "But I'm not sure." He glanced out the window. The weather was still dreary, the way it had been when it had accompanied them on the trip to the house. "But I don't seem to remember constant misting, either.'' Not that that meant a lot, he added silently.

Feeling restless and needing a little space between them, Alison rose and crossed to the same window he'd been looking through. She stared at the beads of moisture on the pane. Rain tears racing one another down to the bottom of the sill. It seemed as if it had rained a little almost every day of her life.

"There's something to be said for that. I'm about ready to leave.''

"The room?''

"No.'' Alison looked at him over her shoulder. "Seattle.''

Leaving. Everyone's always leaving, moving somewhere else. But that's not for me.

The sound of his own voice echoed in his head. But he hadn't said that just now. When? When had he said it? Rousing himself, he realized she was looking at him. Waiting. He tried to pick up the thread of the conversation.

"Where are you moving to?''

She shrugged, letting the curtain fall back into place. "I don't know yet.'' Alison thought of the letters on her desk in response to her inquires. Letters from all over the country and beyond. She had her choice of places, but none felt exactly right yet. "Some place where I'm needed. Some place where I can make a real difference, not just be one of a crowd.'' Crossing back to him, she noticed that he hadn't even attempted to put his hands on the keyboard. Probably didn't figure in prominently into his life, then. The computer enthusiasts she knew took their laptops to bed with them and fell asleep typing. "I've put in applications to various isolated areas where nurses are really needed.''

"Isolated?" The word shimmered in front of him, on the verge of triggering something. He could only hang on for the ride if it did.

"Yes."

It was still out of reach. He needed help, a push in the right direction, but he had no idea what that was. He kept her talking. "Like how?"

She ran the addresses she'd typed through her head. "Like Third World countries, like the Appalachians." She'd seen brochures that wrenched her heart. "There are places even in this country that desperately need medical professionals."

Luc stopped trying to remember. He focused on her. "So you're volunteering."

Volunteers worked without being paid. *Well, wouldn't you almost be doing that?* Alison heard Lily's voice in her head.

"It amounts to something close to that," she allowed. The people who answered her letters tried to paint the best pictures they could, but there was no denying that conditions there made the words *low pay* sound synonymous with affluence because there was really so little that the local residents had. "Room and board, minimum wages, awful conditions." In some cases, running water was a luxury. She hoped she was up to it.

She seemed a little uncertain about it, despite her words. The computer and his own mental odyssey were put on hold. "Then why do it?" he asked.

For a number of reasons. She gave him the most practical one. "To get my credentials."

He had no idea what was involved in becoming a nurse, but it didn't seem to make sense to require this kind of hardship. "Has to be an easier way."

There was. She could have applied to work at a local

clinic, or with someone in private practice. Jimmy had made the suggestion more than once. "I'm not interested in easier, I'm interested in helping."

He smiled. "People in Seattle get sick, too."

That was exactly what Kevin had said to her. She gave Luc the same answer she'd given her brother. "People in Seattle have choices as to who they want to go to. Some of the places I applied to don't even have one medical person to turn to for—"

"A hundred-mile radius." Again, he was echoing something he'd heard, something that had hooked up with the words that came before. Something out of a life he still didn't remember having.

"I was going to say miles and miles, but yes, for a hundred-mile radius, if not more." He had that same look again, as if he were existing on two different planes. "Why do I get the feeling that you're not just second-guessing me?" She studied his expression, wishing she knew how to help. "Do you know one of these places firsthand?"

"Maybe." But if he did, he didn't know he knew. "Or maybe you're just making all this so vivid for me, I can see it through your eyes." He rose from the chair slowly, feeling that same spark again. Wondering why it echoed with loneliness when he did. "You've got beautiful eyes, you know that?"

Lifting her shoulder in a careless shrug, she looked away. Telling herself she wasn't afraid to look into his eyes. "They serve their function."

"They do more than that." Being very careful to only touch the point of her chin, he drew her eyes back to his. "I didn't mean to take advantage of you before."

He seemed so sincere. The fear drifted away. "You didn't."

"Are you sure?" Because he wasn't.

She wasn't eleven anymore. There were times she had to remind herself of that. She'd taken a great many precautions to prevent being in that sort of situation again. She could take care of herself now. Not like then. "If I'd have thought you were trying to take advantage of me, you would have found yourself hermetically imbedded in the floor."

The way she'd raised her chin almost made him laugh. Instinctively he knew that would have been the worst thing he could have done. "In case you haven't noticed, I am more than a little taller than you are. And more than a little bigger."

She'd noticed, all right. Noticed far too much about this man she'd taken into her house. Noticed more than made her comfortable. And now that he'd kissed her...

Nothing. Now that he'd kissed her, there was no change, no impression, no veering off course, she insisted silently. "That can be used against you, you know. Height and weight."

"Martial arts?"

The mind really was a mysterious thing, arbitrarily selecting what it chose to remember and not remember, she thought. "You know about that. Interesting. I feel like I should go trolling through your brain just to find out what else is hidden in the recesses of your mind that you don't know about."

"As long as you promise to be gentle."

She laughed and pointed to the computer. "Just see if anything feels familiar to you." When he merely looked back at the screen, she placed her hands over his and put them on the keyboard.

The electricity that tiptoed through her was unexpected, waking up every nerve ending in her body from point of origin outward. Rousing something formless and shadowy within her, something she didn't understand and didn't want to examine.

"Maybe touching it will remind you of something," she coaxed, trying to keep her voice from sounding shaky.

It reminded him of nothing. But the feel of her hand on top of his stirred that same bittersweetness inside. And there was more. "What kind of perfume is that?"

"What?" When she turned her head, she realized that their faces were much too close. That she was much too close.

"The scent you're wearing." He took a breath and let it fill his head. It soothed the dark corners that existed. "It's been teasing me all day."

Without meaning to, she sniffed. Alison couldn't detect anything unusual. If there was perfume in her clothes or on her skin, she'd long since become oblivious to it. She tried to remember if she'd put any on this morning before dashing out of the house. Nothing gelled. "I don't think I'm wearing any."

Maybe it was her hair that smelled so enticing. Or just her skin. "Then I think maybe you should put a dead bolt on your door because if that's just you, someone's going to try to kidnap you for your secret." The scent was captivating and just the slightest bit distracting. Not unlike the woman herself, he thought.

"I'll take it under advisement," Alison murmured. Tapping the monitor, she drew his attention back to the business at hand. "The computer."

"Yes, it is, isn't it?" He leaned back in the chair, preferring to look at her than the computer. "Why don't you run a program or a game for me and I'll see if anything seems familiar."

It sounded reasonable enough, she supposed. Bringing up the list of programs, she selected a popular one that was dedicated to word processing, thinking it might be familiar to him.

"What do you call it?"

She indicated the top of the screen where the name was written. "That's—"

"No, I mean your hair. What do you call it?"

"Hair?" she suggested innocently.

His smile was wide and engaging. "No, the color. Is it sable? Chocolate? Chestnut?"

She pulled a curly strand in front of her, examining it as if she'd never seen it before. "I don't know, I never gave it much thought. Chestnut, I guess." Her eyes met his. "You're not paying attention."

"Yes," he contradicted, "I am."

The answer made her feel fidgety.

When morning arrived, it found her groggy. Though she'd turned in fairly early, Alison had amassed less than four hours' sleep, having spent most of the night searching for a comfortable spot on her mattress. And failing.

They'd made no progress last night, at least not so far as his memory was concerned. When her brothers came home, they each had tried their hand at prompting Luc's memory, also to no avail. When they finally all went to bed, Luc's past was still a sealed mystery.

But it wasn't his past she was thinking of when she'd gone to bed. It was the very near present.

The kiss they'd shared preyed on her mind, unearthing a multitude of emotions that loomed even larger in the dark. She felt ill equipped to greet another day.

What she needed more than anything was a shower.

As she stumbled out into the hall, she heard her broth-

ers' voices coming up through the vent. They were in
the kitchen, deep in discussion over the Mariners'
chances of making the play-offs this year or at least landing in the wild card position. She heard Kevin complain
that life hadn't been the same since their star pitcher had
left the team.

Good. If they were talking, that meant she would have
the shower all to herself. Neither Kevin or Jimmy could
form a coherent word until after their morning showers.
When it came down to it, none of the Quintanos had
ever been known to hit the ground bright-eyed and
bushy-tailed. It took the combined effort of a cold, bracing shower and a large mug of hot, black coffee to bring
them around to the world of the living.

Right now she felt light-years away from her goal.

Wishing her mouth tasted of something other than
sawdust, Alison placed her hand on the bathroom doorknob and turned it. The door didn't give. Terrific, it was
stuck again. For about the last month or so, the door had
been giving her more and more trouble, and in both directions. She was just as likely to get stuck inside the
bathroom as well as outside it. Busy studying for finals,
she'd asked Kevin, then Jimmy to see about fixing it.
She should have known better.

If you want a thing done…

She'd play handywoman later, Alison told herself.
Right now she needed that shower or she was going to
curl up and die. An extra-cold one. Because in addition
to spending a mostly sleepless night, when she'd finally
fallen asleep she'd had a dream about Luc. It was the
kind of a dream she didn't have. Ever. A warm, physical
dream. Those were for other women who looked forward
to the physical aspect of a relationship, who looked forward to marriage and a happy life.

There'd been a time when she'd actually thought about it, believed she was even capable of it. Of being normal. She felt that all her inhibitions and fears would disappear once she was married. But then she'd married Derek and he'd proven her wrong. The marriage had been a disaster from the moment the vows were exchanged. She'd been a disaster, cringing at his very touch. The whole marriage ran aground within a few months. But only after she'd amassed an endless supply of soul-wrenching belittling that always began in their bedroom and escalated from there.

She didn't need to do this to herself again, especially not when she was only half-conscious, half-capable of warding off the waves of inadequacy that accompanied the memories.

Putting her shoulder to the door, Alison pushed hard. The door flew open.

The next thing to open was her mouth. Wide. The bathroom wasn't empty the way she'd thought. Luc was in it. His presence filled out every corner. He was toweling his hair dry and wearing only beads of water.

For the first time in years, she was completely, utterly wide-awake without the benefit of water. Alison might have been a nurse and accustomed to seeing people without their clothes on, but that was within the framework of a hospital where she was putting textbook knowledge and hands-on experience into play. It certainly had never been within the confines of a steam-filled bathroom in her own home.

The word *magnificent* shrieked across her brain like the whine of a plane breaking the sound barrier.

Somewhere, Michelangelo's *David* was slinking off in shame.

With a strangled sound, Alison pulled the door shut,

blocking out the view and leaving herself on the other side. Her heart was pounding like a drum.

It took her a second to find her tongue and another to get it into working order.

"I'm sorry, I didn't mean to—I was half-asleep—the door—I thought it was just stuck."

She heard him laughing on the other side of the door. Her stomach tightened, clenching. Refusing to let her breathe. How could that sound so sexy to her, given the situation?

It sounded sexy *because* of the situation, she pointed out silently, irritated with herself for stumbling in like that. More irritated with herself because of the reaction she was experiencing. She'd wanted to remain in the room, to stare at him until every hard contour of his muscular body was indelibly etched into her brain.

It probably was anyway.

That man was missing and no one was trying to find him? She couldn't make herself believe that.

A weakness crept into her knees. Needing support, she leaned against the door and almost fell in when it opened again the next minute. Her first thought was that she really should close her eyes.

They stayed open.

Luc's hair was still wet, plastered to his head. The change of clothing she'd given him last night, courtesy of Jimmy, had been hastily thrown on a body that was faintly damp. Everything clung to him. It made him almost as unsettling to look at as he'd been a couple of seconds ago.

He smiled at her, trying to put her at ease. If she were any pinker, she'd look like cotton candy come to life. The way the realization affected him, he figured he had to have a weakness for cotton candy. "It's all yours."

Her mind was a blank. As blank as his probably had been yesterday. "Mine?"

Luc gestured behind him at the room he'd just vacated. "The bathroom."

"Oh. Right." She felt like the embodiment of a dim-witted Valley Girl. "Um, thanks."

Unable to say anything coherent, she quickly closed the door and locked it. The next moment, she moved the hamper up against the door. It wasn't much of an impedance, but it would make a warning noise. Just in case.

Embarrassment was still shadowing her every move when Alison entered the kitchen. Embarrassment for him and for herself. And at what her brothers would say once they got wind of what had happened. If they hadn't already.

Braced, she kept her head high as she walked in.

Kevin and Jimmy merely nodded in her direction, too busy eating to verbally acknowledge her presence. Maybe Luc hadn't said anything.

And then she noticed the table. Instead of the customary toaster waffles or bowls of cereal that they normally had for breakfast, there were huge, plate-sized pancakes, melting pats of butter and absorbing rivers of syrup on each of their plates. Another platter stood on the warming tray Lily had forgotten to take with her when she moved out. The smell permeating the kitchen was heavenly.

Alison glanced around, jumping to the only logical conclusion. "Is Lily here?"

"No, but Luc is." Finished, Jimmy helped himself to a second serving. "Did you know Luc could cook?"

Luc dismissed the enthusiasm in Jimmy's voice. "It's nothing."

"Nothing?" Kevin snorted. "Hell, if you were a woman, I would have proposed by now." Sighing his contentment, Kevin moved a plate aside and reached for the French toast.

Now that she noticed, there were waffles on the counter, too. The kind made from scratch. Almost dreading what the sink had to look like in the aftermath of this cooking fest, she slowly slanted her eyes toward it. And got another surprise. Unless he'd thrown them all away, there were no dishes, no dirty pans, nothing.

The man was a wizard in more ways than one.

He also had that strange look on his face again.

"Luc, what's the matter?" Kevin asked, concerned. Luc's jaw had slackened and he was staring at Kevin in the strangest way, as if he'd just been struck by lightning.

"Hey, I was only kidding about that proposing thing. I didn't mean for you to think that I was—"

But Luc didn't hear him. He was hearing something else, a voice in his head, triggered by what Kevin had said.

The voice belonged to his cousin Ike.

Chapter Six

Like someone caught standing beneath a giant house of cards that had suddenly come tumbling down, everything came flying in at Luc from all different directions. Faces, words, whole sections of memories rushed at him.

He remembered.

Everything.

"Luc, are you all right?"

The voice, melodious and sweet, broke through the elation encasing him. Luc raised his eyes to see Alison looking at him. For just a second, he found himself captivated by the light and the concern he saw in her eyes.

Slowly a smile curved over his lips. The smile of a man who knew exactly who he was again. "I'm terrific."

"Is that you bragging, or—?" Alison's question faded away as the look in his eyes registered. The same empathy she'd felt for him before now brought with it a surge of excitement. "You remember, don't you?"

The grin nearly split his face. Without thinking, he picked her up and spun her around. "Everything."

Exhilarated, he set her down again. It was such a relief, such an incredible relief to have that black drop cloth lifted from around the rest of his life, allowing him to see, to remember. To feel something again besides frustration and bewilderment. Even embarrassment, generated in his not-too-distant past, was welcomed.

Pleased with himself and his earlier diagnosis, Jimmy beamed. "See?" He used his fork to punctuate his statement. "I said his amnesia wouldn't last long."

Obviously her brother was forgetting that she was in the room when he'd offered that prognosis, hedging about the time. "Lucky guess, hotshot," Alison sniffed. But she felt too happy for Luc to carry on the pretense of disdain.

Kevin and Jimmy exchanged curious looks. It was very apparent to both that their sister was elated at this newest turn of events. More so than either one of them would have thought.

"What set you off?" she asked Luc.

"I don't really know," he confessed. It didn't matter how it happened, only that it did. "Something that Kevin said, I think. Suddenly I was hearing Ike's voice in my head."

"Ike," Kevin repeated uncertainly. "You mean like the president? Dwight Eisenhower?"

Luc thought of his cousin, a charmer since the day he was born. Ike would have gotten a kick out of the mix-up. "No, my cousin. Klondyke."

"Strange name for a guy," Alison commented. It

sounded more like something someone would have named their pet.

Luc grinned. Ike hated the formal version of his first name, but it had been the whim of Ike's parents to name both their children after an area strictly associated with their home state. "Not when you live in Alaska."

"Your cousin lives in Alaska?" Alison looked at Luc. It seemed like a whole other world. When Luc nodded, the only logical question followed. "Do you?"

"Yes."

It felt good to remember home and all the things it meant to him. He had always been happy living in Alaska, even though so many of the people in the town, people he'd grown up with, had left as soon as they were legally old enough to do so. Some even younger than that. He had never felt that urge himself, except for a fleeting moment just before he'd left for Seattle. But there had been a reason for that.

"I live in a little town called Hades, about a hundred miles or so out of Anchorage. The only way you can get to it in the winter is by plane. The roads are impassable."

Kevin couldn't imagine living anywhere but in the heart of a thriving city. Wrapping his hand around the chunky glass filled with orange juice, he took a deep swig before saying, "Sounds isolated. No wonder you came here."

"Yes, and got mugged less than half an hour after he landed," Alison reminded him.

"You gotta take the good with the bad," Kevin commented philosophically.

"And this is definitely the good. Well, I for one think that this calls for a celebration." Wrapping up the remainder of his breakfast in a napkin, Jimmy got up from the table. He was late, but that was nothing new. "What do you say? You and me, we can do this city up right. tonight."

"I'd like a piece of that," Kevin chimed in.

Alison looked at her older brother in surprise. Kevin rarely went anywhere but the garage and the house, preferring his entertainment in small doses and restricted to the company of a few good friends. Clubs were Jimmy's domain, not Kevin's.

Jimmy looked more than happy to have Kevin along. "You're in." He broke off a piece of bacon from Kevin's plate, popping it into his mouth. "I've gotta run, but we'll talk when I get off my shift," he told Luc. "We'll take in a few hot spots, make you forget all about Alaska."

"I've had enough of forgetting for a while," Luc told him. "But I would like to see a few things."

"Great. Later." Jimmy was a memory the next moment, hurrying out the front door.

Without realizing it, Alison moved closer to Luc. "If you want to see Seattle, I think the Space Needle would be a good start. Jimmy'll probably only drag you to where his friends go." Out of the corner of her eye, Alison saw Kevin grinning.

"Nothing wrong with that." With a reluctant sigh, Kevin pushed away from the table. "Haven't eaten that well since Lily moved out. Well, time for me to be going, too." He rose to his feet. "I'll see you tonight, Luc. Glad that you're in your right mind again." Tickled by his own wording, he winked at Luc.

Quickly wiping her lips, Alison tossed aside her napkin. She was planning on getting a ride in this morning. "Wait a minute, I'm—"

Kevin glanced over his shoulder, the look in his eyes

freezing her in place. "Going to stay right here and keep our guest entertained. I figure it's the least you can do."

She didn't particularly like having her responsibilities outlined for her, especially not in front of strangers. "I'm driving today, remember?"

"Only if I say so—" He narrowed his eyes, leaving no room for argument. "And I'm not saying so."

She should have known this was coming. Kevin was still overreacting. Nothing had happened to her yesterday. Besides, she could take care of herself. Alison dug in.

"Kevin—"

"Aly—" Kevin teased back. He looked toward Luc, seeking an ally. "See if you can keep her busy today. I'd take it as a personal favor."

Alison's mouth dropped open. Kevin was using Luc to gang up on her. Luc was her discovery, not Kevin's. "But—"

"See you later, kid," Kevin called out from the hallway.

And then it was just the two of them in the kitchen. In the house. The two of them and the memory of his very damp, very firm body, glistening with water beads and looking like every woman's fantasy come to life.

Alison reached for her glass and drained it. She had to get her mind to go beyond that image.

But it didn't.

Her mind seemed to be stuck in Park, the engine revving and thoughts coming at her fast and furious.

Thoughts that didn't belong in a kitchen.

Thoughts that were, she realized, completely out of character for her. She didn't know whether to be glad, or nervous.

Needing something to occupy herself, she began picking up the dishes from the table. For the first time in four years, she had nothing to do and nowhere to be. Freedom felt very strange.

She did her best to sound casual. "So, where would you like to go?"

Luc watched her as she began to wash dishes. Was it his imagination, or was she nervous about something again? "I don't want to put you out—"

"You're not," she heard herself snap, and then bit her tongue. What was the matter with her? "I mean, it's my choice and I want to. Besides, I suddenly seem to be at loose ends today."

Rinsing off the last dish in the sink, she placed it in the dishwasher then turned to pick up the rest from the table. She caught her breath as she bumped into Luc. Alison forced a smile to her lips and took the dish from his hand. Why did the room feel smaller suddenly, as if someone had pushed all the walls in closer?

He looked toward the telephone. "First thing I want to do is call home. I'll reverse the charges—"

He'd come to her rescue, she wasn't about to let him pay for a measly long-distance phone call. "You do and you'll have trouble pushing the buttons after I flatten your hand."

He laughed, wondering if she realized how funny the threat sounded, coming from someone nearly a foot shorter than he was. "I guess the muggers aren't the only ones who are violent in this city."

"Nope." Leaning over the work counter, she pulled the phone closer to them. "Make your call. Your family's probably worried sick."

There'd been no promise of calling on landing, just a tacit understanding that he'd call at some point or other. "I doubt they even noticed. Ike still feels like he's on his honeymoon even though he and Marta have been married for a couple of months now.''

And going at it like newlyweds, he thought fondly. There'd been a time that he'd thought he and Janice would be like that. But that had obviously just been wishful thinking on his part.

Alison waited, but Luc didn't continue. ''Anyone else?''

He thought of Sydney and Shayne. ''Just friends, but nobody who'd expect me to call them when I got in.''

''Oh.'' She didn't realize she was smiling until she caught her reflection in the kitchen mirror as he began to dial.

She took him to see the Space Needle. Because the breakfast he'd made had effectively filled up every available nook and cranny in her body. Even around lunchtime, they only had coffee in the restaurant, taking in the breathtaking view of the city beneath their feet. After that, she brought him to the Kingdome and Pike Place Market. She supposed that she harbored the secret hope of tiring him out so that he'd pass on Jimmy's invitation when her brother came home from the hospital.

But instead of tiring Luc out, traipsing around Seattle only seemed to invigorate him. She supposed that life in the frozen north had built up his stamina and made him heartier than most.

Her subtle plan backfired. At the end of the day she was the one who felt as if she needed a dose of energy. But she'd made up her mind that he wasn't going to go out into the wilds of Seattle's nightlife in Pioneer Square without her. After all, he was from a small town and consequently sheltered. Without saying so, she appointed herself his protector.

One of the duties of a protector, she quickly learned, was being an available dance partner. Luc, it turned out, loved to dance. The fast tempo numbers sapped her energy.

But the slow dances were even harder on her.

She tried not to analyze her reaction and to look, instead, as if she were having fun. She tried so hard, she forgot she was trying.

"How big is Hades, really?"

The question brought a fond smile to his face. He could remember a time when the entire population could fit into one building. But that was before the zinc mine had opened up and industry of a sort had found its way to Hades.

"You could probably stick it in Seattle's back pocket and have room to spare. Just enough people to make a good-size party."

She looked around at all the bodies pressed into the small area that comprised the club. Anyone with claustrophobia would have taken one look and run out screaming by now. "Okay, how many in a good-size party?"

He thought for a second, recalling the statistic he'd read in the weekly newspaper. "About five hundred and three people. A little more if you count the Inuit village on the perimeter."

"Oh." There'd been more people than that in her graduating class in high school. For that matter, there might have been that many people in here. "What do you do there?"

"Until recently, I was part owner of the local saloon. Ike owns the other half," he added. It'd been Ike who'd talked him into the venture in the first place, saying that he needed to do something with his money besides leave it in the bank.

"Until recently. Did you sell out?" Alison caught her tongue between her teeth, wondering if he thought she was prying.

But if he thought so, he gave no indication.

"No, bought in, actually." He saw his answer confused her. Maybe the blow on the head had left him generally inarticulate. He certainly felt tongue-tied at any rate. "The general store." Taking a breath, he backtracked. "The old owner wanted to sell and I thought after the fire, the place could stand a little renovation."

She was trying to piece this all together and not having much luck. "You had a fire?"

"Yes." He nearly laughed. She made it sound as if it was something unusual. Or maybe she thought of Hades as something unusual. That was probably more like it. People generally thought of Alaska as being a million miles away, a place only a little less distant than outer space. "We have fires, parties, births, just like regular people."

This was not coming out right. She did better with a thermometer in her hand, leaning over a bed. "I'm sorry, I didn't mean to—"

His grin was quick, absolving and oddly warming. "Don't apologize. I was only teasing." Luc cocked his head, studying her. "Don't people tease you, Alison?"

"My brothers do, but in general, no. At least, not often enough for me to get used to it." To keep his questions at bay, she forced a smile to her lips. "I guess I've been on the serious side of life for so long, it's hard for me to remember that there are two ways of looking at things."

Because the music seemed to have increased in volume, even though the song was a slow one, he leaned his head in close to hers, whispering in her ear. "Sometimes more."

The press of bodies was getting to her. Both the ones on the dance floor, sucking up the available oxygen, and his against hers. It all conspired to making it far too hot for her to withstand.

She turned her eyes away. That was the easy part. The hard part was anesthetizing her body to the feel of his against it. "So, you're the general store owner and the bartender—"

"Used to be," he corrected. Nowadays he tended bar rarely, only when Ike was away. "Ike handles that by himself now. He's got some hired help, but he likes to spend his time behind the bar, listening to the miners swap stories." He laughed softly. She knew it was crazy, but the sound seemed to glide along her skin. "He tells some himself."

She tried to envision it, to see in her mind's eye a place that was open and friendly, its families' lives tightly interwoven. Sounded almost picture-perfect. And untroubled. "I guess the general store isn't as colorful as the saloon."

He thought of some of the disputes he'd been forced to settle on the spur of the moment. The only difference being that his customers had lists in their hands instead of mugs of ale. "It has its moments. Besides, Mr. Kellogg still works there with his wife."

How much business could there be in a small town like that? "So you're a man of leisure for the most part."

He laughed at the laid-back image that called to mind. A couple bumped into them and he moved over slightly, guiding Alison away.

"Nobody is, in Hades. The weather won't let you be idle." He could see what was on her mind and smiled. Most outlanders thought that way. "We just don't move as fast as everyone else, but we get things done."

It was hard for her to think. It felt as if small, electrical charges were shimmying up and down her body. She wasn't sure if that was a factor of having seen him naked this morning, or just because.

Alison searched for something to keep the conversation going and in the open. "Do you have a hospital?"

He began to laugh then, really laugh. She supposed the question was probably naive sounding at that.

He hadn't meant to make it appear as if he was laughing at her. It was just that he could hear Shayne lamenting the fact that things were still so out of touch in Hades, and it felt good to remember even small things like that. "The closest any of us come to a hospital is when Sydney or Shayne fly us to the one in Anchorage."

"And Sydney and Shayne are—?"

Maybe because of his own dilemma, he said the first thing that popped into his head. "Married." Luc saw the incredulous look that came into her eyes and then realized why. "Sydney's a girl."

"Glad one of them is," she murmured.

Something warm and good moved through him, though he wasn't absolutely sure as to why. He did like the feel of holding her so close, Luc thought.

Luc realized that he was staring at her. But she did have beautiful eyes, even in this lighting. And he'd remembered his first impression of her when he'd opened his on the pavement. He'd thought he was looking up into the face of an angel.

The angel was creating some very unangelic thoughts inside his head.

"Shayne's a doctor," he told her. "And he'd sell his eyeteeth for someone like you."

She tried to take that as a compliment, but something made her stiffen involuntarily. "I take it he's not happy with Sydney?"

"Not happy...?" Luc's voice trailed off as he tried to make sense out of her question. And then he laughed. He was going to have to try to be clearer when he spoke. "Anyone in his right mind would be happy with Sydney. No, I meant because you're a nurse." His tongue grew thicker as he tried to explain. "Shayne needs a nurse. He's been trying to get one to come up ever since his brother left town almost two years ago now. Ben was a doctor, too, but he wanted to get out. Kind of like Ike's sister." He was rambling, he thought. Saying more in the space of these few moments than he customarily did in an entire week. But that was her fault. She was creating this energy within him and he wasn't sure just how to handle it. "They could never get a nurse to come to Hades. Women are pretty outnumbered up there."

That didn't sound right, either. Reconnoitering, Luc pried his foot out of his mouth and tried again. "I guess another way to say it is that women are pretty special up there."

He had a nice way of looking at things, she thought. For the moment, because none of this was quite real to her, Alison laid her head against his shoulder. The music drifted through her, making her sway. Thoughts began linking themselves up in her mind.

Why not?

She raised her head and looked up at him. "Is he really looking for a nurse?"

Why would she think he'd make something like that up? "Yes, why?"

Maybe this was serendipity. She didn't much believe in fate, but there were times when things just seemed to lay themselves out.

"Because, as I mentioned earlier, I'm looking for a place to earn the rest of my credits. I was trying to decide between going to work at this little clinic in Montevideo and a tiny two-man practice in the Appalachians." Both had stirred her sense of charity. But both required a drastic severing of ties. She wouldn't be able to come back home for visits often. "Alaska's a lot closer than either one of them. The flight home wouldn't take nearly as long." She glanced over toward where Jimmy was entertaining not just one, but two women at the table. And Kevin seemed to be getting pretty cozy with the redhead he'd been talking to for a while now. "Not that either one of my brothers would notice I was gone."

He didn't see why she'd say something like that. "Oh, they'd notice, all right. Hard not to notice if someone like you was missing." He cleared his throat, thinking that perhaps he'd gotten too personal. "I know Shayne would be overjoyed to have you."

The more she thought about it, the better it seemed. This was just what she was looking for—a place to make a difference. And there'd be someone there that she already knew. Someone to talk to so she wouldn't feel quite so alone.

She made her decision. "All right, then maybe you could call him tomorrow morning and ask if he hasn't changed his mind."

There was no need for that. He knew Shayne hadn't. Luc studied her for a second. The comparison between Alison and Janice was inevitable. Janice had nothing but contempt for Hades, and here Alison seemed almost eager to go. "You're serious."

"Absolutely."

"This is going to mean the world to him." It pleased Luc no end to be able to be the bearer of this kind of news. Undertaken as a momentary getaway, his trip to Seattle had turned out to be fruitful, not just for Shayne, but for Hades, as well. "Shayne could more than use the help. With three kids to look after, and teaching the local kids, Sydney can only do so much." And then his eyes sparkled with amusement.

"What?"

"Oh, I was just thinking that you've already gotten your feet wet as far as the citizenry in Hades is concerned."

She didn't quite follow. "You mean because I met you?"

The song changed, the tempo stepping up. He continued dancing as if it were a slow dance, oblivious to the people around them and their gyrations.

"No, because you've already seen me in the altogether. The rest should be a piece of cake."

Alison could feel the blush working its way up her cheeks and was grateful that the lighting in the club made reading a menu a challenge. If the rest of the men in Hades looked like him, she had no idea why women weren't overrunning the little town instead of being on the endangered species list.

"Let's not count chickens before we've made a down payment on the incubator. Shayne still has to approve me."

That wasn't an obstacle. "You're breathing, he'll approve. Besides—" he smiled down into her eyes and she felt her knees shifting composition from solid to liquid ''—I can vouch for your gentle bedside manner.''

With effort, Alison squelched the reaction she was having. She looked at him sharply. ''What do you mean?''

''The way you took care of me,'' he explained. He saw the look in her eyes. He'd seen the same kind of look in the eyes of an animal with its foot caught in a trap. He had no idea what he'd said. ''I didn't mean to say anything out of turn.''

She was being an idiot. He was only trying to be nice, nothing more. Why couldn't she just take things at face value? She damned the man who had stripped her of that right, stealing it from her.

Alison shook her head. ''No, it's me. I'm sorry. It's just that—'' She hunted for something plausible to blame. ''Studying for finals has left me a little edgy, that's all.'' Alison shifted gears. ''Why did you come here? On vacation?''

He thought of the letter he'd left on his bureau. ''I just wanted to get away for a few days.'' Without realizing it, he curled his hand tighter around hers. ''Figure out what I was going to do.''

That sounded very abstract. ''You mean with the rest of your life?''

''No, with a problem that's coming home to roost in a few weeks.'' She looked at him curiously. ''I did something stupid.''

He didn't strike her as someone who'd do anything stupid. On an impersonal basis, she felt she was a pretty good judge of character. ''Oh?''

''Yes, I lied.''

He looked so solemn about it, she had to bite her tongue not to laugh. Without realizing it, she relaxed a little. "And I'm guessing that's something you don't normally do."

"No."

That would make him one of a kind. Everyone lied. Some more than others. She was guilty of it herself. "I'm surprised they don't have a statue of you in the Smithsonian."

"Why? Telling the truth isn't that unusual."

The man was an Eagle Scout. "You'd be surprised. What did you lie about?"

He didn't think of himself as reclusive, but he wasn't normally this talkative, either. Maybe it was because he needed to share this, and talking to a stranger was easier than talking to a friend. Especially a stranger with beautiful eyes.

"I told someone I was married."

And that someone counted, she guessed. "An old girlfriend?"

He shook his head. "Not in the way you mean. It was to an old friend who ran off with an old girlfriend. Mine." His mouth curved a little. That sounded almost humorous. It didn't begin to touch the heartache he'd felt, standing there at the altar with his family and most of his friends in attendance, waiting for a bride who never came. "I ran into him in Anchorage about three months ago and we started talking." He hadn't meant for the conversation to go like this, but somehow one word had linked up with another until he'd found himself lying to Jacob. "He told me how happy he and Janice were and I—well, I—"

It wasn't hard to fill in the words. "And you didn't want him to pity you so you told him you were married and happy, too."

It sounded innocent enough when she said it. But now

he was going to have to face up to Jacob with the truth. And look stupid. Served him right, Luc supposed. Still didn't make him feel better.

"Yeah, something like that. I wouldn't have ordinarily but I'd just had a little too much to drink." Even that had been out of character for him. "You'd think tending bar, I'd know not to overindulge, but—" At a loss, he merely shrugged vaguely.

There was a bond between them, a bond that had been formed in that out-of-the-way alley with its dank smells and overflowing Dumpster. She could almost feel his discomfort. And wanted to ease it somehow. "So now you need a temporary wife."

He laughed at the thought. It was something Ike had said to him when he'd asked him about Jacob's pending visit. "Yeah, I guess I do—if I don't want to look like a complete idiot."

The music was still pulsing around them, but she stopped dancing and looked up at him. It only took her a moment to make up her mind.

"Okay."

It sounded like an announcement, or at the very least, an answer to a question. But he hadn't asked anything. Luc could only stare at her blankly. Had he just had a relapse without realizing it?

Chapter Seven

"Okay what?" he finally asked, looking at her uncertainly.

Alison flashed a quick, brilliant smile at him. Kevin had always accused her of thinking faster than she could form words, leaving normal mortals way behind. This was one of those times. "Okay, if that doctor in Hades—"

"Shayne," Luc interjected, more for himself than for her.

She amended her answer. "If Shayne says that he wants me to come up and work with him, I don't see why I can't pretend to be your wife, too." The incredulous look on his face was nothing short of priceless, she thought. It made her feel more comfortable about her decision. "It wouldn't be for a long time, right?" She figured that if they kept the charade up for too long, someone was bound to stumble onto it and ruin things for Luc. But, if it was only for a few days, Alison saw no harm in it.

The music swelled and grew loud again. Luc felt a little the way he had when he was ambling through the maze of amnesia. Not sure where he was going, not sure where he'd just come from.

"No, it'd just be for a couple of days or so. Maybe a week at most." He doubted Janice would want to remain in Hades for longer than that. Rather than pick up the tempo again, he took Alison's hand and brought her back to the tiny table they were sharing with her brothers. "Just what is it that you're saying exactly?"

She didn't think it was that difficult to follow. Maybe his brain was still a little foggy from the blow.

"Well, I feel I owe you. You put yourself on the line for me and you didn't even know me." Every time she thought of it, it still struck her as pretty damn heroic of him. She had her own personal white knight and she meant to repay him somehow. Besides, she didn't like being in debt. Debts had a way of piling up. "The least I can do is to help out when you need a favor."

Accepting her offer would only be compounding the lie. A lie he wasn't comfortable with, certainly not proud of. It was on the tip of his tongue to refuse her. He hadn't a clue exactly what had him backpedaling from his good intentions. But he did.

Debating, he looked into her eyes. "You don't mind doing this?"

"No. It might even be fun."

The way she saw it, this fantasy marriage would be as close as she would ever allow herself to get to being married again. And there was no harm in it. For anyone. She picked up the mai tai she'd ordered and played with the stem of the glass, moving it slowly between her thumb and forefinger.

Her eyes remained on his as she cloaked herself in humor. "So, tell me about this femme fatale who ground her high heels into your heart."

"It wasn't nearly as dramatic as all that." The assurance was offhand.

Perhaps too much so. Alison had a feeling that Luc had a penchant for downplaying things. "Okay, give me the boring version, then."

He grinned at the way she put it, then sobered as he let himself remember. Because it was necessary for self-preservation, he kept the events at arm's length.

"Nothing much to tell. We wanted different things out of life, that's all. I wanted to stay in Hades, work at the business, she wanted me to extend myself, to strive for bigger and better." And to give her the wealthy lifestyle she demanded, he thought.

Alison played devil's advocate, not sure where she was on this. "Nothing wrong with striving."

The shrug was careless, belying the old emotions that still dwelled, in subdued levels, within. "Didn't say there was. But I'd just rather spend the time enjoying what I have. If more comes of it, great. If not, well that's okay, too."

It was, she thought, an admirable philosophy. He believed in smelling the roses along the way. She doubted if there were many men like that around.

"So when you didn't turn out to be the next self-made man/Ted Turner type, she turned her attention elsewhere," she guessed.

Luc took a long pull on the bottle of beer he'd ordered, eschewing the glass mug the bartender had given him. Setting the bottle down, he answered, "Jacob's more her speed."

"And Jacob is—?" When he didn't hear her, she leaned in closer, raising her voice. "And Jacob is—?"

"Was," he clarified. The music seemed to be getting louder and louder. He was practically shouting and growing lonesome for the Salty Saloon. "My best friend. Once."

It figured. "Ah, the plot thickens."

But Luc shook his head. "No plot." It was all pretty straightforward. He didn't believe any of it was intentionally planned. It had just laid itself out a certain way, that's all. "Janice was beautiful and she wanted things out of life I couldn't give her. Things that it turned out Jacob could provide." His lips curved slightly, as he remembered long conversations over fishing poles no self-respecting fish came within spitting distance of. "Jacob always had his eye on becoming bigger than life. Bigger than Hades could contain at any rate."

She detected just the tiniest hint of sorrow in his voice, even with the noise surrounding them. Did he realize that he was still in love with Janice?

"And now Mr. Bigger-than-life is coming back for a visit and you need to show him that you've done well for yourself, too, right?"

"Wrong." Maybe he shouldn't take this any further, he thought. Lies had a habit of complicating themselves. "I don't need to show anyone anything." She looked so interested, he heard himself continuing. "But I did tell him I was married. I don't know how it came out." He knew he was repeating himself, but the whole thing still left him feeling incredulous. "One minute we're just talking, the next minute he's apologizing to me about 'stealing' Janice away and I kind of felt—"

"That he felt sorry for you." A blind person could have seen that one coming, she thought.

He didn't care for pity, never had. To be the object of it rankled him and went against everything he believed in. Luc set his jaw hard. "Yeah, I suppose that was it."

She followed the logical path to the clearing. "So you told him there was no need, that you were happy with—?"

He raised his eyes to hers, God, but he felt silly saying this to her. "Suzanne."

Alison rolled it around in her head, tried it on for size. "Pretty name."

He wasn't sure if she was patronizing him or not. What he was sure of was that he was feeling progressively dumber about mentioning this whole thing. "Look, this was a stupid idea. When Jacob comes, I'll just tell him the truth, that's all."

"Will he rub your nose in it?"

He didn't answer immediately. "No."

Alison read between the lines. "But you're not sure. And you think he'll feel sorry for you."

"Maybe." But that was neither here nor there. And, at any rate, it wasn't her problem. It was his for giving in at a weak moment.

Technically he was a stranger to her. But there was something about him, something that transcended the rules. She didn't want to see him embarrassed. "How often does Jacob come back to Hades?"

"This'll be the first time in three years." And he wouldn't have been returning now except that Jacob had come into some property, land that his father had left him, and he needed to dispose of it.

That cinched it as far as she was concerned. It would only be a one-time deal.

"Okay, odds are that the next time Jacob comes into town, you will be married to someone you really care about." She clapped her hands together, then held them, palms out, signifying a done deal. "You can tell him you divorced Suzanne when you met the love of your life."

He looked at her closely, trying to draw his own conclusions. "And you don't mind doing this?"

"I offered, didn't I?"

Maybe it might work at that. And it was a load off his mind not to be the object of Jacob's pity. Or worse, of Janice's. That was the part he'd been dreading, he realized. It was what kept him from refusing Alison's offer. A man had a certain image of himself. And pity didn't enter into it.

Luc raised the almost-empty bottle of beer to her in a silent toast. "Alison, you're one in a million."

She lifted her head haughtily. "The name's Suzanne—and you'd be the first person to say that."

He didn't see how that was possible, but he had a feeling saying so would only embarrass her, so he kept it to himself. "Well, that's settled. Would you like to dance again?"

She smiled her assent. Taking the hand he held out to her, she rose. "I'd love to."

She felt good in his arms, he thought, a second before he locked the feeling away.

Only the late hour they arrived home prevented Luc from placing a call to Shayne the instant he walked through the door. But he was on the phone first thing the next morning, waiting only to make sure that Alison hadn't changed her mind. She hadn't.

Sydney answered the phone. Luc could visualize her holding one hand over her ear as she held the receiver in the other. Sara and Mac were squabbling in the background. The noise made him smile. Home.

"Sydney, it's Luc. Is Shayne still home?"

"Luc, hi!" She sounded pleased to hear his voice. "You just caught him on his way out. Young Dr. Kerrigan is bailing out of this zoo as fast as his long legs can take him. If you hang on a second, I'll get him for you." She paused to ask, "Everything all right?"

He glanced at Alison, standing next to him, waiting her turn. "Couldn't be better."

"Okay, I'll get him."

Luc heard Sydney call out to her husband and a distant, low voice answer, but he couldn't make out the words. A minute later, he heard Shayne's deep voice saying hello. "Luc, nice to hear from you, although I must say I'm a little surprised you'd call me. How are you enjoying Seattle?"

"Nice city, but I miss Hades. Listen, Shayne, I think I found you a nurse."

There was a long pause. "You're kidding, right?"

"No, I'm very serious. There's someone here I'd like you to talk to." His eyes swept over Alison with an ease and familiarity that took him by surprise. He hardly knew her, yet it felt as if he'd always known her. Always been comfortable around her. He didn't quite know what to make of it. "Her name's Alison Quintano. She just graduated from nursing school and she's—"

Unable to restrain herself any longer, Alison took the receiver from Luc, pressing it to her ear. "Dr. Kerrigan, this is Alison. I'm looking for an assignment to complete my internship and become certified. Luc told me about your clinic in Hades.'' God, would she ever get used to that name? She kept thinking of little red devils every time she heard it. ''I was wondering if I could—''

''Yes!'' Until the word rushed out of his mouth, Shayne hadn't known the excitement that was attached to it. After all this time, he was finally going to have another professional working at his side. But he wanted her to know, at least in part, what she was letting herself in for. Until someone came to Hades, the full impact of the terrain was impossible to prepare for, but he could at least try—without scaring her away. ''The conditions aren't the best here, but we try to stay up-to-date on the latest techniques at least and the rewards of working with these people are indescribable. They really do need a nurse.''

It sounded to her as if she already had the job. ''Don't you want to hear my qualifications?''

''Sure.'' He was getting ahead of himself, but he had been trying so hard for so long to find someone, he could hardly believe it was finally going to happen. ''But your main qualification is willingness.''

''Well, I have that.''

Shayne listened with only half an ear as Alison recited the name of her school, which fields she had more experience in and what she hoped to achieve in the future. The fact that her goal was to become a nurse-practitioner made her an absolute bonanza for him. When she paused for breath, he ventured in. ''How soon can you start?''

Well, that certainly had been easy, she thought. ''How soon do you need me?''

''Last year. No, make that two years ago.''

She laughed softly. He certainly made her feel wanted. ''Then I guess I'd better go pack.''

"Really? Wonderful." Shayne sounded like a man who couldn't believe his good fortune. "Put Luc back on, please."

Alison held out the receiver to Luc. "He wants to talk to you."

Her eyes were sparkling, he thought, taking the receiver. The sight mesmerized him. "Shayne?"

"I don't know how you did it, Luc, or what you told her, but the next baby we have, we're naming after you."

This was the most excited he ever remembered hearing Shayne, except for the time when he'd announced to the entire clientele of the Salty Saloon that he was marrying Sydney. And then the words he'd just heard hit him.

"Next baby? Does that mean that Sydney's—?"

"Yes!" The affirmation was just as enthusiastic as it had been in answer to Luc's first question. "Listen, call me back with her flight number when she makes the arrangements and I'll be there to meet the plane."

"Deal. And I'm holding you to that name thing, you know," he warned his friend. He saw Alison looking at him curiously. "Girl or boy."

"Wouldn't have it any other way." Shayne rang off.

The whole matter had been settled within five minutes. Less. Alison looked at Luc, her heart hammering like the mallets of a percussion soloist. After all this time of endless planning, setting goals, it was all coming together. She was finally going to get her wish and start making a difference.

She couldn't wait.

Alison pressed a hand to her stomach at the sudden onslaught of butterflies. "He sounds very nice."

"What he sounds like," Luc said, moving the telephone back to the center of the table, "is overjoyed." Ordinarily Shayne was a man of even fewer words than he was.

She grinned. "I kind of got the same impression." It occurred to her that, besides her beloved CD collection, she didn't know what to pack. She'd never been away from home before, other than sleepovers as a teenager. Alison threaded her arm through his. "C'mon, you can tell me all about Hades over breakfast. We're going out for breakfast and I'm buying."

It was a simple, small place without the complexities of a large city. "I could probably do an adequate job over coffee."

"I'll eat fast," she promised. Reaching for her purse, she had all but ushered him to the front door when the telephone rang. She knew she could always let the answering machine get it, but it drove her crazy to ignore a call while she was anywhere within the vicinity.

Making a quick dash back, she reached for the telephone. "Hope that isn't your doctor friend, changing his mind."

He laughed. Not likely. "More chance of the end of the world coming in the next three minutes." Pausing, he waited by the front door as she picked up the receiver.

"Miss Quintano?"

She didn't recognize the voice. "Yes?"

"This is Detective Donnelley. I wasn't sure where to call, since we don't have any telephone number, or a local address, for Mr. LeBlanc—"

"He's right here with me." Alison stopped abruptly, conscious of the silent inquiry in Luc's eyes. He crossed the room, coming to her side. "How do you know his last name?"

"Someone turned his wallet into the precinct. It's

empty, of course. No money, no credit cards, nothing except for his license, but at least we know who he is.''

"So does he.'' Shifting her eyes, she looked up at Luc and smiled. "His memory returned yesterday morning. Any leads?''

There was a stony silence before the detective admitted, "No.''

She hadn't really expected any other answer. Crimes like hers went unsolved every day. Even with the partial description of the two men that she had given the detective, there was nothing to really set them apart.

"We'll be right there to pick it up,'' she promised.

"I'll be here.''

Pleased and frustrated at the same time, Alison hung up the telephone. "Pick what up?'' Luc asked the second it sounded as if she'd broken the connection.

"Your wallet. Someone turned it in.'' Impulsively she hugged him, then stepped back. "Looks like things are picking up for you.''

"Yeah, sure does.'' In more ways than one, he thought, following her out.

Kevin sat in his chair, quietly looking at Alison. Outside the small office, the noises of a thriving taxi business continued. Matt was busy putting on new brake shoes on Car 3, and two of the regulars were off to the side, playing cards until the cabs they were assigned to came in.

But none of that penetrated his office. There was an eerie silence within the small enclosure. Alison had just come by to tell him her news. Luc was outside, giving them their privacy.

Kevin appreciated the gesture.

He wished Luc had never come into their lives.

Kevin sighed, running his hand through his dark, curling hair. He'd always felt very protective of Alison. To a greater or lesser degree, that feeling extended to all his siblings. But it was more intense with Alison. She had always struck him as the one most in need of him.

Oh, he knew she tried hard not to be, to display a confident, tough exterior to the world, but he wasn't fooled. He knew better. He was her big brother. Underneath all that bravado, that verve and zest, there was a scared little girl.

The same little girl he'd found cowering on the floor of the closet of her room, crying her eyes out all those years ago, right after their father had died. Crying and refusing to tell him why. It had taken hours of patience, of simply holding her, talking to her and waiting for her to trust him enough to tell him what had affected her so badly.

He'd thought it was because she missed their father. But that hadn't turned out to be the case.

It had taken two of his friends to physically restrain him and keep him from killing the man with his bare hands when he'd found out. A man who had professed to be a family friend all those years, who'd come to help them get over their tragedy in their time of need. And who had, instead, compounded that tragedy.

And now she was going off on her own, hundreds of miles away where he couldn't take care of her any longer. He realized it was inevitable and even for the good. At least he knew that was what he was supposed to believe. But he didn't have to like it any.

Kevin made up his mind then and there not to have any kids of his own. This kind of thing hurt too much.

He studied her face. She looked determined. More

than that, she looked eager. "Are you sure about this, kid?"

"Very sure." She could talk to Kevin the way she couldn't to the others. Talk in fragments and knew he'd understand. "I'm scared and excited and happy, all at the same time."

Happy was all he wanted for her. "How soon are you leaving?"

"Well, school's over and I seem to have lost my part-time job." She smiled at the face he made at her. She knew he meant well, even when he was restricting her. Kevin always worried about her and she loved him for it. Most of the time. She paused, knowing that he wasn't going to like this part. "Day after tomorrow."

"Day after tomorrow—" Stunned, Kevin stared at her. It didn't even give him time to catch his breath. He supposed it might even be better that way. Like a quick injection instead of a long, drawn-out inoculation. "That fast?"

She nodded. "The doctor up there really needs someone." Her tempo increased with each word, as if the faster she talked, the easier it would be to convince him. "I'll be the only nurse. It'll be a great experience and I'll finally get to matter."

He rose then, looking at her. "You've always mattered."

She swatted a hand at him, muting the sentiment shimmering between them. "You know what I mean."

"Yeah, tough guy, I know what you mean." Her mind was made up, he could see that. He didn't mind admitting, in his heart, that he had hoped that she could find someplace close by to carry out her vocation. He knew all about her desire to go to out-of-the-way places, knew all about the letters that were coming in from the four corners of the world, vying for her, but he'd still gone on hoping. "We'll have to throw you a goodbye party at Lily's."

He'd never know what his silent approval meant to her. "I'd like that." Relieved that was over, she turned to leave.

"Consider it done. And, Aly?"

She glanced at him over her shoulder. "Yes?"

His words came slowly, measured, each with its own field of emotion. "While you're up there in this godforsaken place on a stick, if you ever find yourself needing anything, I mean *anything*, just pick up that telephone and call me. I'll be on the next flight."

She pressed her lips together. "I know you will. And I appreciate it, big brother."

Turning, and throwing her arms around Kevin's neck, Alison hugged him, blinking back tears. She didn't raise her head to look at him, not because she didn't want him to see her cry, but because she knew he didn't want her to see him doing the same.

Chapter Eight

Holding two glasses aloft, Luc made his way out from behind the four-sided bar in the center of Lily's main dining area. It took a little maneuvering not to bump into anyone.

The doors had been closed for this private party. It was almost as crowded within the small, upscale restaurant as it had been at the trendy club Kevin and Jimmy had taken him to three nights ago. But, unlike the club, here the noise was genial, almost soothing. There was a warmth generated by these people who had come to see Alison and the stranger who was taking her off with him on a brand-new adventure, to a little town not one of them had heard of before today.

He knew none of these people, had only met Alison's sister, Lily, when he had arrived with Alison earlier, yet for the space of the evening, they had all accepted him into their wide circle. They were treating him like a friend, one of their own.

It made him think of the Salty and Hades, where everyone, whether they knew one another to only nod at, or to carry on a daily relationship with, was invisibly and irrevocably linked to everyone else.

The pang went right through him. Sharp, deep, sweet. He was homesick, he realized. It felt good to have somewhere to miss. To remember missing somewhere. And someone. But this time, it was family and friends he missed. Not like the other time, when Janice had left him.

He'd even given a ring to Janice. Nothing fancy, but it had been his mother's and there was a world of sentiment attached to the small, antique gold band. He'd found it, along with a note, on his dresser after the wedding was to have taken place. His best man had left everything in his wake, taking his intended instead. Janice had left, she wrote, with Jacob, because he was a man who had vision. The news had hit him with the force of a tsunami, completely flattening him. Flooding him with hurt and anger, and a gut-wrenching feeling the depth of which he had never even vaguely admitted to, not even to Ike, although he had a feeling the latter had suspected.

The anger had been the first to leave. In time he had grown to miss Janice less, to be less hurt. And in the place of all those feelings had come a wariness, a sense that he could never care again in that way, *would* never care again in that way. The interlude with Janice had created invisible bars around his heart, dedicated to preserving his pride, his dignity and his feelings.

He'd thought them invincible. He wasn't a hundred-percent sure of that anymore.

Approaching the table where he, Alison and her family were sitting, he saw her. And heard her. The sound of Alison's laughter came to him like a soft, sensual, undulating wave. Reaching him, it began at his toes and moved upward with the unexpected thrust of an incoming tide. Slowly, then quickly, building momentum until it reached its peak.

He waited until it passed, then continued on his odyssey to the table.

Would she regret giving all this up? Leaving these people she obviously cared for so much and going off to what amounted to the end of the world? He knew she had said she was looking for somewhere to make a difference, to apply her skills and make them count for something, but he knew there were times that rhetoric and reality were two very different things.

How homesick would she get?

Well, he thought, moving around a couple so deeply involved in a conversation they were oblivious to everyone else, it would be something they would both find out in time. With luck, he'd be there to help her over the bumpy parts.

He finally made his way to their table. "Oh, you did get the drinks." Smiling at him, Alison reached for hers. "We thought maybe you got lost."

"No, it just took a while, that's all."

Lily, a taller, slightly older version of her sister, glanced over her shoulder. For most of the evening, she'd been alert, the consummate hostess, but just these last few minutes she'd allowed herself to be merely Alison's sister, sharing her on her last night home for who knew how long? The alertness was back in her eyes as she looked toward the bar. "Bill's not usually so slow."

"He's not. But he looked beat, so I said I'd cover for

him for ten minutes while he took a break. I made these." Luc set his own glass down, then took the vacant chair beside Alison. She'd been holding it for him, he realized. "And a few others, as well."

There were seven orders in a "few." The bar was far fancier than what he was accustomed to at the Salty, but the basic stock was the same. And he'd known his way around a bar ever since he'd been in his midteens and Ike had talked him into working with him for the Salty's owner. Until eventually they had become the owners. That, too, had been Ike's idea.

You always need a fire lit under you. I can't keep lighting them, or waiting for them to light. I want a man who's going places, who wants to give me things. That had been part of Janice's note, too. He'd wanted to give her things, but the kinds of things he'd wanted to give her hadn't involved money as the bottom line.

Lily's brow drew into a reproving frown. "Hey, you're the guest of honor here along with Aly. You shouldn't have to be doing any of the work." Studying the man behind the bar, she realized Luc was right. He did look tired. Probably coming down with something. She hoped it wasn't catching.

Lily rose, pushing back her chair. Bill could probably use a longer break. "Duty calls." She smiled at Luc. The man wasn't afraid to help out without waiting to be asked. That spoke well of him. Maybe Alison was going to be all right after all.

Bending, she brushed a quick kiss against his cheek. "Thanks for pitching in. I appreciate it. But you should have called me, or hauled Jimmy over. He knows his way around an order." Jimmy had worked as a waiter all through medical school and taken his turn behind the bar, as well, when the need arose.

Luc only grinned. There was no point in going into his own past. "He looked busy."

Scanning the crowd, Lily picked Jimmy out. He was on the far side of the room, surrounded by three women. So what else was new?

"He's *always* busy that way." Her eyes slanted toward Alison and Luc before shifting to Kevin. "Speaking of busy, why don't you make yourself useful and feed the jukebox some money so these nice people—" she gestured around the room "—will dance instead of eating me out of house and home."

Kevin reached into his pocket and pulled out a handful of change. He deposited the coins on the table, spreading them out in order to pick out the quarters. "Dancing stirs the appetite for some, you know."

Lily deliberately avoided looking at either her sister or Luc, but her inference was still clear to Kevin. "Maybe I'm counting on that, too. Start with 'Moon River.'"

"'Moon River'?" Luc repeated, puzzled.

"Slow number," Kevin told him. He scooped up the quarters in one hand, dropping the rest of the change into his pocket. "One of Lily's favorites." He made eye contact with Luc, leaving. "Alison's, too."

He looked at Alison. It seemed to him that the crowd around them was drawing back. He leaned in closer to her so he didn't have to raise his voice to be heard. "I didn't think you were the type to like old music."

She lifted a shoulder in a half shrug. "I don't mind it one way or the other. But that particular song reminds me of my dad."

He noticed that her eyes grew a little misty as she spoke.

"He used to play it a lot. Said it was his and Mom's

favorite.'' Blinking, she chased away the sadness and kept only the sweetness. "They danced to it at their wedding. When I hear it, I remember sitting on the floor in the den, coloring, while my dad worked on his lesson plan. Kevin said he was a hell of a teacher.'' She sighed. "I don't remember that part of it. I just remember 'Moon River.'" The music began to fill the room, reaching her above the pleasant din of voices in the background. Her eyes were stinging again. She looked away. "It always makes me feel a little sad to hear it now."

He wasn't sure what to do, only that he didn't want to add to her discomfort. "Would you like to dance or just sit this out?"

There was no hesitation. She was on her feet immediately. "Dance. If I'm moving around, maybe I won't get too sloppy."

Taking her hand, he brought her away from the tables. Her body fit so well against his, it was hard to imagine that they hadn't always been like this. Hadn't always danced together. He looked into her eyes. And felt a smile forming within him.

"Can't picture you sloppy."

She laughed softly. The sound flirted with his stomach muscles, tightening them before he ordered them to relax.

"Thanks, I needed that. I guess I'd better keep you away from my brothers, then. They'd be more than willing to give you an earful of all my shortcomings. Especially Jimmy."

He glanced over toward where he had seen the other man earlier. Like them, Jimmy was dancing. There was a redhead in his arms and a blonde a breath away, looking as if she meant to cut in at any second. He sincerely doubted that Jimmy could be torn away right now to give him a litany of Alison's faults, real or imagined.

He liked them, he thought. Liked all of them. They were good people. Concentrating, he could remember Jimmy treating him in the E.R. "What's your brother's specialty?"

Alison followed his line of vision, although she knew he wasn't asking about Kevin. Her mouth curved fondly. "Women." As far back as she could remember, there had always been girls following Jimmy around, calling at all hours, turning up on the doorstep, wanting to see him. And though she'd teased him, he'd never really allowed it to go to his head. "But if you mean medically, he's got his sights set on being an orthopedic surgeon. Right now, he's practicing by setting broken hearts instead of broken bones." She turned her attention back to Luc. "Why? Are you thinking of recruiting him, too?"

He looked at her, trying to decide if that had just been a random choice of words. "Is that what I did with you, recruit you?"

She shook her head. It was hard concentrating, when the music was whispering to her like this. Making her feel things.

"No, I guess you didn't. I recruited myself. But I don't think the frozen North holds much appeal to Jimmy. Especially if there's a shortage of women." She leaned her head back, her hair brushing against his arm. "Don't get me wrong. He's dedicated and all that, but he really likes to have his fun, too." She paused, pensive.

"What is it?"

She looked away again, this time laying her head against his shoulder. "Nothing."

Something small and warm moved through him, A wisp of smoke curling through his veins.

"I don't think so. It's something." She made no answer. He didn't like the idea of something bothering her. If she had doubts about this huge step she was about to take, he wanted her getting them out in the open now, while there was still time to change her mind. "One of the skills I developed tending bar in Hades is listening. I'm pretty good at it now. And at being able to tell when someone's not telling the truth."

She raised her head and looked at him. "I was just worrying—thinking," she amended quickly.

"Second thoughts?"

It was too sweeping a term. "Not about the work."

"The place?"

She bit her lower lip, wondering how far to let him in. Wavering between not at all and just a little bit. "The people."

She seemed to get along so well with everyone here, he couldn't imagine her worrying about getting along with anyone. "I can vouch for a good many of them myself." It wasn't that, he thought, studying her face. But it was something. "What about the people? Specifically."

She tried again, telling herself not to freeze up. Feeling that iciness anyway. "I was just thinking—you said there was a shortage of women—maybe—"

It was as if her thoughts telegraphed themselves to him in clear, precise sentences.

"Nobody clubs you over the head and rushes off to the nearest cave, if that's what you mean." He thought of the way it'd been when Sydney had arrived. Men tripping over themselves and each other to make her feel welcome. "It's kind of the reverse, really."

"You're going to have to explain that one."

The song had ended, but Kevin had obviously thought it deserved an encore because it began again. "They'll all vie for your attention. Shayne'll probably suddenly have twice as many patients as he usually does, for a while." That, too, had happened when Sydney had pitched in to help him at the clinic. Shayne's brother, Ben, had left almost two years ago and everything had been chaotic ever since. "All coming to look you over. All coming to hopefully be looked over."

The explanation didn't seem to help. He felt her stiffening ever so slightly, saw the uncertain look in her eyes. It made him think of a kitten that had been mistreated and was afraid to draw near to the hand that was stretched out toward it.

"Nobody's going to play tug-of-war with you." His hand tightened around hers protectively, though he hardly realized it. "For one thing, nobody's going to let anybody get ahead of them that way. It'll be kind of like a system of checks and balances." God, but she looked beautiful in this light. "And for another—"

Though she couldn't explain why, she felt as if she were alone with him. As if there was no one else but them within the room. Within the moment. "And for another?" she coaxed when he didn't continue.

"I won't let them." He paused, then forged ahead, knowing he had no gift when it came to talking. That was Ike's department. Ike had the silver tongue. As for him, he was more of a doer, when things needed doing. "You're kind of my responsibility."

She raised her chin ever so slightly, independence coming to the fore even while something small within her rallied to his promise. "I can take care of myself."

He hadn't meant for her to think he thought otherwise.

''I know that, but Alaska's a whole other ball game. I'm just going to hang around in case you need some of the rules explained.''

She cocked her head, the light catching the tiny diamond studs at her ear, sending out flashes everywhere like tiny rainbows. ''Rules?''

Maybe *rules* wasn't a good word. ''Things you should know,'' he amended. ''Like you called it the frozen North a few minutes ago. That's only in the winter. Right now, it's hotter there than it is here probably.'' He was willing to bet on it. ''And there's about two minutes of nighttime. That makes up for the fact that six months from now, there's almost nothing but night.'' He stopped, wondering if he'd scared her off. He wasn't exactly painting the best picture of the place. God, but he wished Ike was here. Ike liked Hades as much as he did. Ike would have been able to present it in its best light, glossing over its drawbacks instead of highlighting them.

He didn't want to scare her away. He wanted her to come.

She appreciated his honesty. Above all else, honesty had always been important to her. She relaxed again, softening in his arms. ''I grew up in rainy Seattle. I can handle gloom.''

He nodded, then pretended to be serious. ''But can you handle perpetual sun?''

Her eyes danced. ''I guess we'll just have to see, won't we?''

Luc had the strangest sensation that he was being taken captive, without ever having heard any shots being exchanged. ''Yeah, I guess we will.''

He felt it.

What's more, Luc hadn't realized he was feeling it

until it was there beside him, nudging him, demanding his attention.

He was attracted to her.

And, what was better—or worse, depending on his point of view—his attraction gave every indication of something that was in the middle of gestation. It was growing, blooming.

Except that it shouldn't. He didn't want it to. He'd been there, involved up to his heart in a relationship that he firmly believed was one thing when it was completely another. The upshot of it all was that he'd gotten his teeth kicked in and his heart demolished. He had no burning desire for that to ever happen to him again. Once was quite enough, thanks.

Besides, this wasn't about attraction, not for her. She was going because of some noble purpose she felt she was fulfilling. To boot, she was going to be doing him a favor, trying to save his pride. Another noble sentiment. Giving in to feelings that were scrambling around in him like so many laboratory mice looking for the right path, would be no way to pay her back.

And yet...

And yet all the common sense he was attempting to infuse into his brain seemed to disappear the moment they arrived in front of her house. The noise the car doors made as they were closed echoed through his head, pulsating. Adding to the beat that was going through him.

They were the only ones out on the street.

Kevin had remained at the restaurant to help Lily with cleanup. Luc and Alison had volunteered to lend a helping hand, but Lily had refused, saying it was their party, not their mess. And Jimmy had gone off to cover for the person who had covered for him so he could attend the party.

That left him alone with Alison. And with a fresh outbreak of attraction.

He walked her to the front door, feeling like an awkward teenager. "Your sister certainly knows how to throw a party."

"That's *her* specialty," Alison told him. "Lily loves to throw parties, loves to organize." A smile winked across her lips. She was missing her family already, and she hadn't even left yet. "Likes to order people around, too."

"Well, good night."

He saw that same vulnerability in her eyes again, the one that made him want to protect her. The one that stirred him, churning up other emotions. Like desire. He thought he could stave it off with just a quick kiss goodnight.

He thought wrong.

All the fleeting touch of her lips did was add new life to the growing attraction he felt rather than satisfy it. When his lips brushed hers, he wanted more.

But that was his problem, not hers. He kept himself in check. Because he didn't want to frighten her after all his talk of her being his responsibility, and because she'd stiffened the moment the kiss had given the slightest hint of being just this side of intimate. One moment, she was leaning into it, the next, she was ramrod straight and backing away. For one brief second there'd been terror in her eyes.

Why?

"Alison, I'm sorry, I—"

Her hands shook just a little as she jammed the key

into the lock, twisting it quickly. "That's all right. I'm just tired. I'll see you in the morning."

The next minute, the front door was closed and she was gone.

Feeling confused, Luc shoved his hands into his pockets and walked back to the garage. But instead of going upstairs, he sat down on the bottom step. The night air was still, except for the crickets that were vainly trying to summon one another.

Luc stared out into the darkness, trying to clear his head and sort things out. He wasn't quite sure what was going on with either one of them.

That was where Kevin found him half an hour later, sitting on the bottom step, still staring out into the darkness, no closer to an answer than he had been when he'd first sat down. The only thing that had changed was that the stars had faded, giving way to the clouds.

Kevin came around the side of the garage. "What are you doing out here? It's starting to rain."

Luc looked up, not at Kevin, but at the sky. He hadn't felt the rain until Kevin had mentioned it. "Kevin, can I ask you something?"

There was something in his tone that gave Luc away. "It's about Alison, isn't it?"

"How d'you know?"

He paused, leaning against the wooden banister. "Women aren't the only ones with intuition." He didn't add that he'd watched them dancing together and, that in unguarded moments, his sister looked as if she were happy. He hadn't seen that look about her when she'd been with Derek. Kevin turned up his collar against the pregnant mist. "Okay, what's the question?"

He wasn't sure how to put it and not give Kevin the

wrong idea. "Is there someone Alison's leaving behind?"

The question surprised Kevin. He hadn't anticipated that. "You mean, other than her family? Like a boyfriend or something?"

"Yeah." Maybe that was why she seemed so easy to be with one minute and so stiff the next. God knew it wasn't because he was a threat. No one had ever seen him as a threat. Maybe there was someone in her life and he wasn't around right now because they'd had an argument or something. Maybe she was having doubts now because of him.

Kevin shook his head. "No. She hasn't had a boyfriend since her divorce."

Luc looked at him in surprise. "Divorce?"

"From the sound of your voice, I guess she hasn't gotten around to mentioning that she was married to Derek. Not that she probably will. She doesn't talk about that much." He didn't blame her. The way Kevin saw it, it had been a mistake from the moment the vows had been exchanged. Even before that. Derek hadn't been worthy of her, although he supposed in the man's defense, Derek hadn't understood what he was getting himself into. "It was a quickie thing, over before it started. I'm not really sure why she ever married that guy. I don't think she was, either. I always had a feeling she was trying to prove something to herself." He was talking too much, he thought. Going places only Alison had the right to take Luc. He shrugged, dismissing his words. "But whatever it was, she didn't prove it. She just found out that one mistake doesn't erase another."

Luc's brows drew together. "Another?"

Kevin glanced at his watch. "It's getting late. You'd better get some sleep if you're catching the early-morning flight. For that matter, so should I.'' He clapped him on the back. ''I'll see you in the morning, Luc.'' He started to walk away, then looked over his shoulder. ''Oh, and by the way, I'm holding you personally responsible for my sister. Anything happens to upset her, I'm coming after you. Just a friendly warning. Good night.''

Luc wasn't sure if the man was kidding or not. ''Good night,'' Luc murmured after a beat. Shaking his head, he got up and slowly went up the stairs. To spend most of the night awake.

*   *   *

Chapter Nine

The trip from Anchorage's airport to Hades had been smooth and swift, passing quickly. The wind had been with them. Luc found himself hoping it was a good omen.

He was the first one out off the small Cessna, opening the passenger door the moment the plane had stilled. Very carefully he scanned the area, trying to see it through eyes that were other than his own.

It wasn't easy. He had always loved Alaska, loved Hades, but he knew firsthand that his feelings were in the minority. This was a place that people left. He and Ike and Shayne had remained, natives from the first. Natives till the end. But they had all had friends, lovers and family leave. Ike's sister, Juneau, had wanted to leave from the start, and when Ike had tried to talk her into staying, she'd run away. Even though she hadn't managed to leave the state, she had left Hades as far back as she could. Alaska affected a lot of people that way, making them yearn for something different, something more.

On others it had the reverse effect. Shayne had tried to conduct a practice in New York City, but his heart hadn't been in it. It belonged out here.

And Luc supposed he and Ike had tried in their own way to modernize the little town. It was an uphill battle. While Hades had electricity, phones and running water, and even a movie theater now to call its own, it was light-years away from being thought of as the next hub of civilization. Civilization came to places like Hades to rest, to rejuvenate and to remember where it had come from.

Luc realized that he was just the slightest bit nervous, wanting Hades to put its best foot forward for Alison. There was no way to make the town seem any better than it was. For him, in any stage, that had always been enough. But what about Alison?

The thought had haunted him since last night. He felt responsible for her coming here. And for any disappointment she might be experiencing, now and later. If he hadn't told her about it, about Shayne, she'd still be home with her family.

And poring over letters from places just as out of the way as Hades that were clamoring for her, he reminded himself. It might as well be here than there. Here, at least, she could start out with a friend. And quickly make more.

Luc looked at her now as Shayne jumped down from the pilot's side. They'd landed near Shayne's house. The way the land sloped made it easy to see Hades from here, especially from Alison's vantage point as she stood on the threshold of the plane's entrance.

He tried to read her expression.

Alison shaded her eyes, squinting into the horizon. She could make out rectangular shapes in the distance.

Was that it?

It had to be. There was nothing else around for miles that even vaguely fit the description of a town. She looked harder. It looked like a doll's village. A cluster of buildings huddled together for company, and not all that many buildings at that. The entire town looked as if it could be wrapped up in a handkerchief and tucked away for safekeeping.

Squinting even more, she saw dots here and there which, she supposed, might represent other people's houses. These people liked their open spaces, she thought. It looked as though there were miles between properties. She didn't know if she found that picturesque or desolate, but that was something she figured she'd find out.

Alison jumped when she felt someone taking her hand.

He hadn't meant to scare her. She looked whiter than the mountain peaks in winter.

"The first time I saw Seattle, I thought I'd been dropped headfirst into a blender—set on high." His eyes on hers, he helped her down. "It'll grow on you and sort itself all out in time."

"I'm sure it will." Although there didn't seem to be that much to sort out, she added silently. There appeared to be more homes in her one development than there were in the entire town.

A pang of homesickness assaulted her. She fought it back. She was very proud of herself for not giving in to tears, especially when she'd seen them shimmering in Kevin's eyes. Even Lily had cried, and Lily never cried.

But she had remained strong. She wasn't about to break down, not in front of Luc.

He was still holding her hand. Alison looked at him, somewhat surprised that he was sensitive enough to pick up on her unease. She'd patted herself on the back for having masked it well. Obviously she'd patted too soon.

On the ground, she turned toward Shayne who was unloading her suitcases from the tiny cargo space. "Is the clinic far from here, Dr. Kerrigan?"

It was a short drive and in the summer, without hazard. "Not far, and if you're going to be working for me, you'd better get used to calling me Shayne. It takes too long to say 'Dr. Kerrigan.' By the time you get it out, the emergency's either over or the patient's bled to death." There were only two suitcases and he picked them both up, glancing from one to the other before looking at Alison. "This doesn't look like much." Did that mean that she was only willing to give Hades a cursory try?

She'd never needed much. Her CD collection and audio set would be coming under separate cover. There wasn't anything else except for an album of photographs. Possessions had a way of entangling a person, cutting into their freedom, and freedom, she'd come to believe, was the greatest possession of all.

"I'm having the rest of it sent once I know where I'm staying."

Shayne surrendered one suitcase to Luc, but kept the other himself. He turned toward his house and began walking.

"The local hotel is still undergoing reconstruction." He didn't add that the building was experiencing a moratorium because there were no funds to complete the work. That sounded much too negative. "Until we can come up with a better arrangement, Sydney and I thought you might want to stay with us.'' He thought of mornings at his house. There were battlefields that were quieter. ''That is, if you don't mind noise.''

She smiled, remembering home and her siblings. None of them could have ever been accused of backing down from a good fight. ''Noise'll be fine.''

It would help fill in the empty spaces left vacant by her family's absence, she thought. This was going to be a huge adventure for her, hopefully one from which both she and the place she was working in would profit. But right now, homesickness was still playing a rough tug-of-war with her emotions, and she welcomed any distractions that came her way.

''Then you're in for a treat,'' Shayne promised, ''because, especially with the baby, we've got noise to spare.''

''Baby?'' Alison's eyes, Luc noticed, lit up like a Fourth of July sparkler. ''I love babies.''

Pleased, Shayne looked over her head at Luc. ''I think we have ourselves a winner.''

Luc gave a slight nod of his head, his lips only curving slightly. ''Looks like.''

The slight inflection she caught in Luc's voice both warmed and frightened her. Knowing it was futile, Alison tried to hang on to the one and block the other.

The door of the house they were approaching suddenly swung open. Two children, a boy and a girl, came spilling out, followed close behind by three adults. Alerted by the noise of the approaching Cessna, they were coming to greet Hades' newest citizen.

The two women directly behind the children waved. Shayne waved back.

''Looks like the welcoming committee's here.''

There was affection in Shayne's voice as he warned her. He was obviously referring to his wife. She thought it nice to have someone in love with you to the extent that it overflowed into his voice when he spoke.

She hurried to keep up with the two men on either side of her. "I want to thank you for coming to meet me—us," she corrected.

"Thank him?" The tall, ruggedly handsome man who was as dark as Luc was fair, hooted as he came to join them. "Shayne would have driven all the way down to Seattle to bring you back if he had to. You're all he's talked about since Luc called the other day." He winked. "You'd think that he was going out on his first date instead of waiting for his nurse to arrive." In an exaggerated, courtly fashion, he presented his hand to her. "Welcome to Hades, darlin'. I'm Ike LeBlanc, Luc's cousin. This gorgeous woman standing beside me is Marta. My wife." It still tickled him to say that. He figured to an extent, it always would.

Marta, a petite blonde, laughed as she leaned past her husband and shook Alison's hand. "Don't let Ike throw you. He can be a little overwhelming at first."

Ike took his wife's unguarded moment as an opportunity to brush a quick kiss against Marta's cheek. "Why, thank you, darlin'." Something only slightly removed from a good-natured leer crossed his face as he looked at her. "So, I overwhelmed you that first time at the airport, did I?"

"Hush." For good measure, Marta placed her fingertips to his lips to silence him, not trusting Ike to listen to the simple command. He grinned and kissed them, causing her to be momentarily at a loss what to do with him. Except to love him, which she did with all her heart.

"And this lovely creature is *my* wife, Sydney." Still holding one suitcase, he slipped his other hand around Sydney's shoulders. Just a little more than eighteen months ago, Shayne Kerrigan would have sworn to anyone that he didn't have a demonstrative bone in his body. It had taken Sydney to make him see otherwise. Now it was as natural as breathing to affectionately kiss his wife in public. "You look tired. Snowcone still fussing?"

"Snowcone?" Alison echoed, confused. "Is that your dog or your cat?" Or did the name belong to a more exotic pet, like a baby seal or a moose?

The little girl covered her mouth to seal back an attack of giggles.

"Neither," the dark-haired boy told her solemnly. "That's our sister." Twelve, he was trying very hard to be twenty, and was, to anyone with eyes to see, the very spitting image of his father.

"And she's fussing 'cause her teeth are coming in," the little girl chimed in, not to be outdone. "She cries a lot. Not like Ce-Ce."

"Celine's our little girl," Marta explained.

Alison's head was beginning to spin, trying to keep everyone straight.

"Snowcone—Virginia," Sydney amended, coming to the defense of her littlest one, "doesn't cry a lot, just intensely. But that runs in the family." Humor graced her mouth as she glanced at the two children before her. And then she looked at Alison. "Hi, I'm Sydney and you must be Shayne's godsend. Welcome to Hades."

Not standing on ceremony, Sydney embraced the younger woman. There was something in the girl's eyes that brought out the mother in Sydney. But then, lately, she'd noticed that everything seemed to be bringing out the mother in her. As the doctor's wife and the mother of both his children and their newest addition, Virginia, Sydney felt as if everything as far as the eye could see had been left in her care. She took to the role voluntarily and with gusto.

Stepping back, she smiled at Alison. "God, but we are glad to see you."

"You are gonna stay, right?" The instant her mother released the newcomer, Sara slipped her small hand into Alison's, taking command. She began pulling her into the house, as if entering the building would render her a permanent citizen. "We need ladies out here. Mama said so. And Daddy's almost been praying for a nurse. I'm gonna be a nurse when I grow up, but Daddy said he couldn't wait that long. Do you like it here?"

Ike looked at his watch, then at Shayne. "I clocked her at two hundred words a minute. How about you?"

"Close," Shayne agreed.

"Stop teasing her," Sydney told them. "And as for you, Sara, let the lady catch her breath. She's tired." Sydney's eyes shifted to Alison. "Right?"

"No." The answer was quick, automatic. It was her stubborn streak, Alison realized, taking over. Never admit frailty or vulnerability of any kind. It was a credo she hung on to as fiercely as a starving dog hung on to the only bone he had. "I'm fine, really. And I plan to stay here for at least a while, if things work out."

"What things?" Sara wanted to know.

"Sounds like a budding reporter, doesn't she?" Shayne asked, leading the way into the house.

"A healthy dose of curiosity's a good thing," Alison said.

Sara knew she and the new lady were going to be great friends.

Gently but firmly Luc disengaged Alison's hand from

Sara's grasp. He gave the surprised girl a quick smile. "She needs to put her things away." With Alison's hand in his, he turned toward Sydney. "Which one's Alison's room, Sydney?"

"End of the hall." She pointed to the right of the staircase. "It's just off the kitchen," she apologized. "We were going to give you the upstairs guest room, but that's right next door to the baby and we were afraid she'd keep you up all night."

"Off the kitchen will be fine," Alison assured her. "That means the smell of coffee, first thing in the morning." Her eyes shone. Just like back home. "Perfect."

Luc saw Ike and Shayne exchange approving glances. A ray of pride pushed forward. He knew that Alison was supposed to be nothing more than an acquaintance, but he was glad they liked her. Glad she seemed to be fitting in so quickly. Out here, a person needed to see the bright side of everything in order to survive. There were plenty occasions for nature to try to show you the darker side.

Moving around Mac, who was watching Alison very intently, Luc led the way to the back of the house and Alison's room.

She paused in the doorway, looking in, before slowly venturing into the room. It was half the size of the one she had left behind. There was a dresser, newly refinished, against one wall and a double bed with the most inviting comforter she'd ever seen covering it. A throw rug handwoven by the housekeeper, Asia, covered the space between the bed and dresser.

Sydney came in behind them. There was hardly space for the three of them, much less Sara who was attempting to squeeze in. She bit her lip. Maybe the upstairs guest room would be better.

"It's a little crammed," Sydney allowed.

Alison turned around to face her, nearly bumping into Luc. "Cozy."

"I like this girl—sorry, woman," Shayne amended, depositing her other suitcase beside the one that was already on the bed. "You're going to fit right in here just fine."

She hoped so. At least for the duration she was going to be here, she thought.

"Okay, everyone out," Sydney announced. Turning, she began to herd Sara and Mac out. Mac looked particularly disgruntled since he was just trying to come in. "You, too, Shayne, before we all suck up the available air and Alison asphyxiates."

Muttering words of encouragement, or complaint in Mac and Sara's case, they left the room. Except for Luc.

"Need any help?" He indicated the two suitcases.

The word *help* always got her back up, before she could stop herself. She crossed to what she took to be the closet.

"I've been hanging up clothes since I was old enough to reach a hanger," she replied, turning the handle and opening the door. "Provided they have...hangers." There were several spread out over the rod. She was in business. "What more could I ask for?"

It was clear to him as she snapped open the locks on her suitcases, that he was only getting in her way. Luc took his cue with grace, beginning to back out the door. "Okay, then I'll leave you to get acquainted with everyone."

He nearly backed up into Ike, who was poking his head into the room. "She can do that at the party tonight."

Alison stopped hanging up the jeans she'd taken out

of the first suitcase. Her eyes went from Ike to Luc. "Party?"

"Sure, in your honor." The people in Hades used any occasion as an excuse to get together and socialize. A newcomer to their midst was plenty reason to celebrate. Ike saw the hesitation in her eyes. So, under the bravado, she was shy, he thought. "You've gotta come, darlin'. Everyone'll want to meet you."

She'd made her peace with the prospect of having an assembly line of men moving through Shayne's office under one pretext or another, solely for the purpose of looking her over. Luc had already forewarned her of that. Besides, there was her position to shield her. But meeting them all in a party atmosphere was another matter entirely. One she wasn't sure if she was comfortable with.

At the same time, she didn't want to seem standoffish, either. She was going to have to live among these people for at least a while. Longer if this proved to be her niche.

Telling herself she was creating problems where there were none, she tried to remain calm. There was safety in numbers, right? "And where is this party supposed to take place?"

"Where we hold every party in this town—at the Salty," Ike answered. There was pride in his voice as he said the name. "Part saloon, part clubhouse, it's the local meeting place. Luc and I are joint owners."

"I can come by to take you," Luc offered, forgetting that it was not only logical, but easier for Sydney and Shayne to bring her with them when they came, and that she wouldn't be needing a ride.

To his surprise, Alison nodded. "I'd like that." Just then, she thought she heard a small, lusty wail. She looked at Luc. "Is that—"

"From the sound of it, it's Snowcone," Ike confirmed. "Celine has a deeper cry."

"It's been known to shatter glass," Luc put in.

"Only because you dropped it," Ike reminded him. "He's not much on crying babies."

"Spoken like an expert," Luc countered. "Up until a few months ago, he was more likely to clear the bar with a diaper than to properly put it on a baby's bottom."

Ike crossed his arms before him. "I am really going to enjoy seeing you as a father someday."

The words brought back the memory of wounds not totally healed and promises that were broken. "Then you've got a long wait ahead of you, I'm afraid."

She felt as if she'd stumbled into a personal conversation, one she shouldn't have been hearing. She knew Luc's words were motivated by what he'd gone through after Janice had jilted him. What kind of plans had he made with her, she wondered.

None of her business, she reminded herself. She'd gone through her own hell with Derek, except that she'd been the one who hadn't kept promises. Not that she hadn't wanted to, but that she couldn't. She just couldn't.

Don't go there, her mind whispered.

Rousing herself, she looked at Luc. "Do you think Sydney would mind if I took a peek at the baby?"

"Mind?" Ike laughed. "Why, darlin', nothing she likes better than showing that little beauty off." He looked at his cousin. "Why don't you do the honors, cousin, and take the lady to see Snowcone?"

"Why does everyone call her Snowcone? Is she very pale?"

Luc laughed. "No, the first time Sydney took her outside, it started to snow very lightly and a snowflake landed on her cheek. Sara said she looked like a snow-cone and the nickname stuck.''

Sara was standing immediately outside the door, lying in wait for her new friend. She rolled her eyes dramatically at her sister's crying. "She's at it again."

"That's the only way babies have of getting our attention," Alison told the little girl.

"That, and grabbing hair," Marta agreed. Celine was at that stage now, where every random strand that came into her range was a temptation.

"Would you like to come up and see the babies?" Sydney offered. "Celine is upstairs with Virginia."

"I'd love to see them," she enthused.

"Then come on." Sydney hooked her arm through Alison's. "It only gets worse."

"Nice job, Luc," Ike murmured as he watched the women, closely followed by Sara, go up the stairs and disappear down the hall.

Shayne recognized the tone in Ike's voice for what it was. Admiration, pure and simple. He had no worries about his best friend. Ike was head over heels in love with his wife. But there were a great many unattached men in and around Hades. Men who would melt at the sight of a woman far less attractive than the one Luc had brought home with him.

He looked at Ike pointedly. "Pass the word around that anyone does anything to scare her off, they'll have to answer to me personally."

"And me," Luc added quietly. The other two men turned to look at him. "Well, I'm the one who brought her here. I didn't tell her about this place to feed her to the wolves."

"Nice save," Ike commented.

Luc wasn't sure if he liked what Ike was implying. "It's the truth."

Ike merely smiled easily. Indolently. "Whatever you say."

He didn't want his cousin getting the wrong idea. "Hey, I'm not looking for anyone. Is that clear?"

Ike knew all about that kind of defense. It was made out of tissue paper. Wet tissue paper. "Haven't you heard? That's the best time. It usually finds you when you're not looking."

Luc wasn't following. "What does?"

"Fate."

It wasn't the word Ike wanted to use, but Luc looked a little touchy around the edges. And his cousin had been through a lot these last few days, not to mention before then, when the letter from Jacob had arrived. Since he didn't want to start an argument, Ike thought it prudent to fudge the truth a little. He figured that in his heart Luc knew what he was talking about. And the heart was the organ that mattered in this case.

Luc merely frowned, dismissing his cousin's words as the ramblings of a man in the throes of a happy marriage. He was glad for Ike, maybe even a little envious, because he felt that the odds were against him ever being in that kind of a relationship. Especially if he didn't intend to venture forth emotionally.

But he'd made his peace with that a long time ago.

Chapter Ten

"And I thought the club where Jimmy took us was packed." Alison looked around and shook her head in wonder. It was wall-to-wall people no matter where she looked within the popular saloon. "Just how many people can you fit into the Salty?"

Luc laughed. The throng was so thick, it was difficult to see the wall decorations they had accumulated over the years. The accompanying din made talking without shouting a challenge.

"Probably a good deal of Hades if we wanted to. The Salty's the town's main recreation area and the old owner built it to accommodate everyone who lived here at the time."

Someone accidentally bumped Alison from behind and she found herself pressed up against Luc. The unexpected contact sent spears of warmth through her, tipped in pleasure. Before her mind caught up and brought rigidity with it. She did her best to move back and pretend that there hadn't been a sudden upheaval within her.

She gestured around the room, careful not to hit anyone. "So this represents a population explosion."

"Of sorts. And here comes some of the old population to meet you." Luc put their conversation on hold while he went through yet another round of introductions as Hank Black Arrow presented himself before them.

Part Native American, part Inuit and part Russian with a smattering of French thrown in for good measure, Hank had been around for as long as the Salty had been serving liquor, and appeared not to have aged any in that time. To Luc, the man had been old then, and was old now, but somehow no older. It was as if, in Hank's case, the alcohol was acting as a preservative.

Small, sharp dark eyes looked Alison over with an amused, appreciative gleam before Hank nodded and shuffled off to claim another beer. He hadn't said a single word.

She watched Hank get absorbed by the crowd. Someone caught her eye and raised a tankard to her in a not-so-silent toast. It was the third time tonight. "From the mute to the verbose. They're a colorful bunch," Alison announced.

Luc saw where she was looking. "That's one way of putting it." That was Yuri with the raised tankard, he noted. "Don't let them get started telling you stories—you'll be here forever. Nothing these men like better than a new audience—unless it's a new female audience."

He couldn't help allowing himself his own quick scrutiny of Alison. She'd worn a simple, off-the-shoulder dark green blouse and a pair of snug-fitting jeans. Had there been a war on, she would have been what all the men would have been fighting for, he mused. And maybe he would have numbered in their ranks.

Turning he saw another cluster of men at the bar. These were closer to Ike's age. Seven in all. "I think you already have yourself a fan club."

He gestured with his mug toward a section of the bar where the men were all facing in their direction, their eyes unabashedly on Alison even as conversation occupied their tongues. It was easy to see that the men liked what they saw.

Something protective stirred in him even while he was tolerantly amused.

They'd been here about two hours, and in that time it seemed to Alison that every single male who could walk or hobble had come up to her to be introduced, most had not been as silent as Hank. There'd been a handful of women, as well—wives or daughters of the aforementioned men. But by and large, it appeared as if Hades was predominantly a man's town. Luc had warned her about that, but part of her had thought he'd been exaggerating.

Apparently not.

She wasn't sure if she could get accustomed to that. To having so many men around. It made it difficult to relax.

It amazed him that he could almost read the thoughts moving across her brow when she looked away from the bar. "That make you uncomfortable?"

Her head jerked up. "What?"

"Being looked at." He took a sip, passing the tip of his tongue along his upper lip to denude it of the wisp of foam that hung there. "I'd think by now you would have gotten used to it."

She realized she was staring at him, at the way his tongue had just flicked across his lips. Alison took a deep breath before asking, ''What makes you say that?''

He shrugged. He would have thought that self-evident. ''When a woman's as outstandingly beautiful as a black orchid, I just assumed...''

The comparison stunned her. ''A black orchid?''

She was staring at him as if he'd just said something that defied comprehension. ''You know, one of those really rare flowers—''

She didn't need him to explain what a black orchid was. She'd had a friend with a hothouse who reveled in growing them. They required an infinite amount of patience. ''How would you know about black orchids?'' That hadn't come out quite right. ''I mean—''

He knew exactly what she meant, but he tolerated it with a good-natured smile. ''The nights are long here. I read. You'd be surprised what you can pick up in books. And now, with the Internet—''

Someone bumped into her again, and she covered the mouth of her wineglass with her other hand to keep the contents from splashing on Luc. In two and a half hours, she'd still hadn't finished her first glass.

''You have a computer?''

He took no offense, but it was hard not to laugh. ''Yes, the aliens passing through on their way to the Delta Quadrant left off one for me.'' He grinned. ''This isn't *really* the end of the world, you know. That's only a figure of speech.''

He watched the light pink color quickly progress up her cheeks and then spread down her neck to the opening of her blouse. He found it arousing.

''I'm sorry, I didn't mean to make it sound like... I guess I was just making uncalled-for assumptions. The men here are miners, the population mix is off balance, I just thought…''

He cocked his head, helping her out. ''That we ate with our hands and used our knives and forks to scratch ourselves?''

''No, but, well…'' This was getting worse instead of better. This time, she drained the remainder of her glass, stalling. Maybe it would even help. She couldn't do any worse. ''Can I start over?''

He shook his head, taking the empty glass from her and placing it on the table. He had to brush up against her to do it. It was a hardship he could live with. ''No, I kind of like that shade of pink on your face.''

She had that coming, she thought. ''Comes from chewing on my foot.''

He pretended to look down at the ground, and her foot. ''Can't have that. You'll sink into the snowdrifts in the winter. We do have a lot of that. Snow,'' he tacked on in case she'd gotten lost.

Alison blew out a breath. Was it her, or had it gotten incredibly hot in here in the last couple of minutes? She glanced toward the window. Daylight was still streaming in, despite the late hour. ''You also have a lot of sunlight. What time is it?''

He couldn't see his watch, but he knew they'd been here over two hours. ''Time for the moon to be up if you were back in Seattle. We're coming close to the longest day in a few days.''

''The longest day.'' It had never had much meaning for her back home, although she did like having more daylight available to her. She liked the sun; it made her feel safer. But being in a den of predominantly men negated that. ''What do you get then, about a minute's worth of night?''

"About," he teased. Looking at her, being close enough to be a stand-in for her shadow, was making his mouth turn suddenly dry. "Sorry you came?"

"No," she answered truthfully. "Just trying to get oriented."

That, he knew, was going to take her a while. Just as long, he judged, as it was going to take him to get oriented to having her around. But it wasn't going to be a task he minded undertaking.

A couple of miners began filing by, their drinks held aloft to keep them from spilling. The one closest to him gave Luc a thumbs-up sign. "We're with you, Luc. All the way."

The other man, older of the two, had his eyes glued on Alison. "Mighty nice stand-in you picked for yourself, boy. Ask me, she's worth ten Janices. You got the better end of the deal. Janice got Jacob."

The two men laughed at the miner's joke as they continued the journey to their table.

They hadn't been the first to voice their support since they came in. Jean-Luc LeBlanc must have been one hell of a well-liked man for the entire town to be willing to lie for him.

"Looks like you've got the locals behind you." She turned toward the bar, or tried to. "Is everyone in on this?" she asked incredulously. That meant roughly five hundred people, if she were to take him at his word, were willing to lie for Luc.

What sort of charisma did he have, what kind of sway to elicit this kind of cooperation? Back in Seattle, she would have been hard-pressed to cite a time where this many people would have been in agreement over anything, except maybe the weather.

"For the most part," he told her. He saw the look of

awed disbelief in her eyes. "Ike told me he passed the word around. Bored people are willing to do anything for diversion."

He was being modest. You didn't see much of that around these days, she thought. Especially not where men were concerned.

"Seems to me that more's involved here than just boredom. They wouldn't be doing it if they didn't like you a great deal. I didn't think you'd have this many friends." She pressed her lips together, hoping that the noise had swallowed up her last sentence.

"The people in Hades are a close-knit bunch." Inclining his head closer to her, he asked, "Why?"

Alison made a short, futile stab at playing innocent. "Why what?"

"Why wouldn't you think I'd have this many friends?" Up until now, he'd never thought of himself as off-putting. Did she?

Alison lifted a shoulder, looking away. Feeling awkward. "You're so soft-spoken, so easygoing." She felt his hand cupping her chin, turning her face toward his.

"Again?" He hadn't heard her. She repeated what she'd said, raising her voice a little. He didn't know whether to be amused or offended. "And what, only loud, hyperactive people have friends?"

Somehow, amid people bumping into them and moving around them, she and Luc had made their way to the bar. She took another glass of wine and paused for a fortifying sip before continuing—and hoping to do better. She couldn't remember ever tripping over her tongue this much before.

"No, but outgoing people usually have more than non-outgoing..." She bit her lower lip, looking far more appealing than she knew. He found it difficult to draw his eyes away. "This isn't coming out right, either."

He decided to go with amusement. "That's okay. I'll spot you. No penalty if you start over again."

"Okay, I will." She blew out a breath, grateful, then tried again. She raised her head, smiling at him. The thought that he had kind eyes crossed her mind. "It's nice to have so many friends."

Luc glanced around, but his mind was only on the person in immediate proximity. Alison could be included in that group she was referring to because she'd volunteered to undertake this charade without any prodding on his part. He wondered if she considered herself his friend.

His eyes held hers for a moment. "Yes, it is."

Ike came up behind them. Laying a hand on each of their shoulders, he looked from one to the other, then focused on Alison. "Having a good time?"

"Yes, thanks." The answer was automatic, but she meant it.

"Anything I can get you?" Technically he'd thrown this party; that made him the host, though Shayne and the others had insisted on splitting the costs. It seemed like the miners were able to consume their weight in beer.

She glanced at all the people milling around or standing in clusters. Her head felt like it was swimming. "A roster so I can keep all the names straight."

"That'll come in time," Ike assured her, and then he winked. "They've all got your name straight. If I were you, I'd be looking to see half these faces at the office tomorrow. It'll give you a second chance to remember who's who." His grin widened as he picked out his friend from the crowd. He was talking to Marta. His wife seemed very animated. He wondered what was up. "And give you an opportunity to watch Shayne grumble."

"Shayne?" She couldn't quite make herself believe that. The doctor seemed so mild-mannered. "Grumble?"

Ike nodded solemnly. "Second nature to him. When Sydney first came, she helped pitch in at his clinic and the men were lined up clear out of the waiting room into the street. Didn't please Shayne one iota." He winked at her again. "Forewarned is forearmed, darlin'."

She wasn't sure if anything could really forearm her for this crowd.

Luc glanced at the clock on the rear wall in the general store. Eleven-thirty. Time for a break. He'd been working for the last four hours straight and he needed to stretch his legs.

Especially in the direction of the clinic.

It wouldn't hurt to see how Alison was doing. After all, she was his responsibility....

He stopped himself. The sentiment was beginning to sound a little old, even to him. But it was true. He *was* responsible for her, no matter what anyone else might think. Good or bad, she wouldn't be here if it weren't for him.

Good for the town, he thought. But it remained to be seen if it was good for her. There were times last night when she'd seemed a little edgy to him, as if she were waiting for something to spring out at her. He would have guessed wild animals, except that whenever she did seem edgy, wild animals didn't even remotely enter into the picture.

Only he did.

Luc shrugged. He was probably just imagining it.

Probably for her it was just a holdover from the mugging.

Shoving his hands into his pockets, he walked out.

It didn't take him long to see it. There was a line all right, a big one. It snaked out of the clinic, with men sitting down and around on the wooden porch, waiting for their turn. Whether with the doctor or with Alison, he wasn't sure. But he had a hunch.

The mine had to be at a standstill.

Luc shook his head as he approached the squat, one-story building. "Haven't seen so many sick people in my whole life," he said to nobody in particular.

Nonetheless he got answers.

"Well, now that we've got ourselves a medical team, it don't hurt to have things checked out."

"Yeah, like that little nurse."

"Wouldn't you like to have that little piece of heaven served on toast for breakfast?"

Luc swung around so fast to face the man who'd said that that the miner felt as if he was in danger of swallowing his tongue. Issac Wales held his hands up in mute surrender. "Just a joke, Luc, just a joke. We know she's yours."

Luc's eyes narrowed. "She's not mine," he corrected tersely.

The man at his elbow came alive. "Then she's fair game?"

Damn it, maybe it had been a mistake to let Alison come here. "She's *not* game." There was a warning note in his voice. "She's a lady. And if any of you forget that, you're not going to like the consequences."

They had never seen Luc so outspoken, so protective.

Boris Ivanoff cleared his throat? "Make up your mind. Is the woman spoken for or not?"

She wasn't, but saying so to this crowd might bring about something tantamount to a stampede. Discretion was the better part of valor, especially in this case. "That's up to the lady."

His answer didn't have the desired effect. Instead, the men seemed to take that as a challenge.

There was no sense in talking to them until they'd settled down. Shouldering his way inside, Luc saw her immediately. Alison was moving from the reception desk to the back room where Shayne had called her to assist with an inoculation. She looked harried, but she was glowing at the same time.

She'd been serious when she'd told him she wanted to make a difference, he thought. Anyone could see Alison seemed to thrive on the energy being generated.

Maybe it might work out at that. She could probably handle herself with these men. None of them posed a threat in the real sense of the word. And if anything got out of hand—he'd be there to take care of it. He owed her that much.

She didn't know how she knew he'd walked into the clinic. God knew there were enough people to mute his footsteps and any telltale movements. And her back had been to the door just now, yet she'd known. Something seemed different—the air, the noise, something. Something that told her he'd come in.

She offered Luc a smile of greeting as he crossed to her. "Don't tell me some mysterious malady's come over you, too."

The preponderance of complaints this morning had encompassed general aches and pains that couldn't be pinpointed to any real source. They'd lasted long enough to allow the sufferers individual sessions with the doctor—and her—before leaving the office. It seemed to be enough.

Luc hooked his thumbs in the corner of his pockets. "No, just here to see how it's going for you."

They'd been busy from the moment they'd entered the clinic. "If it were going any faster, it'd break the sound barrier. I thought you said that things were laid-back and slow around here."

"Usually are." But they hadn't gotten used to her yet and wouldn't for a while. After that, he figured things would get back to normal. "And they will be again, in about a month or so." He glanced around the waiting area. They were standing two and three deep. "After these jackasses tire of trotting in here."

Shayne came out of the office. It was evident that his tolerance was being stretched to the shredding point. He held up an empty serum bottle in one hand and a syringe in the other.

"Any more of you here for your 'tetanus booster,' we're fresh out of serum." None of the men had ever come in for a tetanus inoculation, no matter how much he lectured that they should keep up on their shots. It looked as if Alison had accomplished some good her very first day, he thought. "Won't get any in until I make the run to Anchorage at the end of the week." Sarcasm wove through his tone. "My advice to the rest of you is to be careful at what you're doing for a change. Unless you want lockjaw."

"Seems to be they've already got drool jaw," Ike commented, walking in. He noticed that none of the men were leaving. Obviously another ploy would do just as well as the one they'd just been deprived of.

Shayne sighed. "You, too?" He thought he could have counted on at least Ike not stopping by.

"No, I just came by to see if your new nurse wants to be sprung for lunch. Marta sent me to serve as a one-man rescue team if need be." He purposely sidled up to Alison. "How're you holding up, darlin'?"

Alison's eyes swept over the men before answering. "Terrific. I like keeping busy."

"Then you're in luck," Shayne told her. "Because we hardly ever lack for something to do around here." He looked at Ike and Luc, then indicated the door. "Now, if you two department store mannequins will clear out and leave the professionals to the work at hand—"

But Ike merely slipped an arm around Alison's shoulders. It surprised him when she stiffened, since she'd been playing along up to now. "You don't want to be accused of working this poor girl to death, now, do you?"

"Woman," Luc interjected. "They like to be addressed as women."

Alison moved aside and turned to face the two cousins. "'They' like being addressed by their name even more. And 'they' hate being referred to in the third person when they're standing right there in front of you."

Luc saw her point and acknowledged it. She was right. "Sorry."

"Hey, she's got you henpecked already," one of the men in the far corner of the room hooted. He nudged the man next to him. "Looks like he's got this married routine down pat."

Ike raised an amused brow. "Well, if he doesn't, he knows that he can come by your place and take notes, right, Paddy?"

The men around him laughed. Annoyed, but unable to dispute what was being said, Paddy shut his mouth.

Moving her slightly aside, Luc turned his back from the reception area and lowered his voice so only Alison could hear. "Seriously, if you'd like to stop for something to eat, we could go back to the Salty now." He glanced toward Shayne who was busy ushering the next patient in. "You get to have a lunch hour."

"No, thanks anyway. I'll eat later. There's too much to do." She wanted to get the feel of the place, to turn the clinic's routine into her own. This was her very first medical office out of nursing school, and she wanted to leave her mark on it. Most of all, she didn't want to have Shayne regret hiring her.

Luc nodded, leaving. "Up to you."

He returned fifteen minutes later.

Luc had gone back to the general store where he'd taken some of the goods he stocked and made her a salad with a side order of a beef-and-turkey sandwich. He'd been toying with the idea of putting in a lunch counter in the general store's alcove. Not to compete with the Salty but to act as a compliment, allowing people a quiet place to eat if they wanted it. He knew some of the women in Hades would welcome a place to eat out away from the boisterous noise made by the miners when they frequented the Salty. Expansion, he'd come to realize, had its place within the scheme of things, even in a place like Hades.

He brought her lunch and a can of soda pop on a tray. Because he didn't want to deal with any comments from the men in front, Luc used the back entrance to the clinic. Walking in, he surprised Shayne who'd just stepped out of one of the examining rooms.

Shayne saw the tray and smiled. "You can use my office if you'd like."

He didn't want to give Shayne the impression that he was waiting for her. For that matter, he didn't want Alison to think that, either. He was beginning to see that that sort of thing made her uneasy.

Stepping into Shayne's office, he set down the tray and backed out again. "Just tell her it's there when she needs it. I've got to be getting back."

Shayne nodded. "Whatever you say."

This, he thought, watching Luc leave, was going to take time. But then, all good things did. He grinned to himself. Wait until he got home and told Sydney. For once, he was going to have the drop on her when it came to gossip.

Chapter Eleven

"**O**f course he likes her. Any fool could see that." Stopping to look at him, Sydney patted her husband's face with affection. He was so cute when he tried to be in the flow of things. "Not that you're a fool, darling, but you can be pretty oblivious to what's going on around you at times."

He followed her around the kitchen as she got dinner ready. It was Asia's granddaughter's birthday and Sydney had given their housekeeper the day off. Indignity at the slur goaded him. "Name one."

Sydney closed the refrigerator and raised her eyes to his. Humor danced in them. "All right. The way I felt about you."

She had him there. He frowned, refusing to go down without a fight. "Name another."

She laughed and kissed his lips quickly before turning

back to the roast she had promised the kids. "Don't get me started, Shayne, I've got too much to do."

Shayne sank down on a chair, automatically taking the potatoes that were destined to eventually be mashed, and began peeling. "So everyone knows?"

Sydney shook her head. "No, not everyone. I don't think he knows."

"He?"

"Luc."

"Oh." That didn't make much sense to him, but he figured he was out of his depth here. Deciding not to touch his wife's observation with a ten-foot pole, Shayne continued peeling the potatoes instead. It was safer that way and a great deal less confusing.

She should have worn a hat, like Sydney suggested. It was just that wearing hats had never been something she'd done, even in the winter. And this was summer, after all. Summer with the summer sun beating down on her head, making her almost unbearably hot.

Alison passed the back of her hand against her forehead, wiping away the perspiration that had formed, and frowned at the fishing line. It had been hanging this way, off the pole and into the water, perfectly still, almost limp, for what felt like forever. Long enough for the sun to probably turn her chestnut hair to an off-blond.

She glanced at the man who was sitting only a few feet away from her. Half lying was a more accurate description. Luc looked as if the fishing pole he held in his hand was merely an afterthought, not the primary reason they were supposed to be out here.

When she blew out an exasperated breath, he looked over in her direction.

"Are you sure I'm not doing anything wrong?"

A smile slowly curved his mouth. That was the city in her, he thought, wanting everything done yesterday. That wasn't why they were here. He'd thought coming here would be a pleasant change for her from the hectic clinic. After almost two weeks of getting acclimated, he figured she could do with the break.

"It takes patience." For her benefit, he sat up. "Sometimes the fish bite and sometimes they don't." He indicated the empty spot beside him on the grass. "I haven't caught any, either. You were the one who wanted to try this." He'd suggested it, leaving it in the realm of "someday." Alison had been the one to turn "someday" into "now"—just like he knew she would.

"I know, I know." She wasn't blaming him. "I just thought it'd be more productive, that's all."

Productive. It was a word he associated with the world outside this small piece of earth. Something Janice might have espoused, he thought. It wasn't that he didn't like being productive, or progressive, it was just that he saw no reason to let himself be ruled by it.

He nodded at the stream. A range of mountains stood reflecting themselves on the other side. All in all, it was an idyllic scene. One that inspired peace within the viewer.

Most viewers, he amended, looking at Alison again.

"This is part of that laid-back thing I was telling you about the other day. You're supposed to enjoy relaxing." His eyes indicated his pole. "The fishing is secondary."

She liked succeeding at what she tried. Almost needed to. She ran her tongue along her lower lip. He probably thought of her as pushy, but she couldn't help it. "What if I needed to catch fish to eat?"

His eyes swept over the barren space reserved for her catch. Humor deepened. "Then you'd have a problem."

He wanted her to enjoy herself, not to become frustrated. That negated coming here. "Look, if you'd rather just call it a day—"

She held her hand up, stopping him. She shouldn't have said what she had.

"No, you're right. I'm here to enjoy myself and see what people in Hades do for recreation besides sit around at the Salty—or gather in the doctor's waiting room to look over the newcomer."

Word had it that that was dying down. So far, from what he'd heard, Alison hadn't accepted any of the invitations that had come flooding her way. The verdict was that she was shy and would come around eventually. If there was one thing the men in Hades had, it was patience.

"They do a lot more of the former than the latter." Although, truth be told, he could understand spending hours staring at her. She moved like poetry and made a man think things he shouldn't.

She gave a vague lift of her shoulder. She couldn't really complain; everyone had been exceptionally nice to her. "Guess it's only natural to be curious about a stranger."

She wished she didn't feel so unsettled when he looked at her. After all, it was normal to look at the person you were talking to. It was just that she could almost feel his eyes on her face, on her skin...

Alison shook herself free of the feeling. "So tell me about your plans for the general store."

He could almost see her shifting gears and wondered why she felt the need to.

"Nothing much, just what I said the other day." He didn't normally like to put his plans into words until he was absolutely sure about what he was doing and more than halfway there. But he'd found himself telling Alison about his idea over dinner the other night when Sydney had invited him over. "I was thinking of putting in a lunch counter for mothers and their kids."

From what she'd seen so far, unless patrons came from the Inuit village beyond the outskirts of town, that didn't amount to exactly a large crowd.

"Won't do much business," she commented.

He didn't have to consider his answer. "Enough. Besides, the object isn't to 'do business' or make money, it's to give people a choice." Years ago, he remembered hearing his mother complain that there wasn't anywhere for a woman to go to be with other women without having a man at her elbow. This could be that kind of place. "Ike and I practically grew up in the Salty." He saw the interest in her eyes and heard himself continuing. For a private person, he'd been doing an awful lot of talking these days. "Our fathers were brothers and they liked spending their time there with their friends. If we wanted to spend any time with our fathers, we came along."

It had seemed like a nice enough place, but there was still that connotation hanging on to it. "And your mothers didn't mind?"

The question caught him off guard, then he realized what she had to be thinking. "It's not a bar, it's a saloon." There was a world of difference between the two. "Like a pub in England. A place for friends to get together and talk, play a little pool, shoot some darts, things like that."

She couldn't help laughing. "You almost make it sound like a public service."

That was one way to describe it, he supposed. "Maybe."

She shifted on the bank, the muscles in her rear beginning to cramp a little. Without realizing it, she shifted closer to him.

"Then why have the counter in the general store?"

What he was proposing made her think of photographs she'd seen of the old-fashioned five-and-dime with its lunch counters tucked away in the corner. She saw no need for it if the Salty was as genial a place as he maintained.

"The Salty's for everyone, but since we've got a lot more men than women, it's more of a guy's hangout. The counter, like I said, would be for women when they want to get together away from men." He figured that would make the most sense for her.

She could relate to that far more than he'd suspect, she thought. Cocking her head, she studied his face. The man was full of surprises. "Nice of you to think of something like that."

He merely shrugged and looked away. Compliments always made him uncomfortable. He saw her line moving. "Hey, I think you've got a tug on the line."

Even as he alerted her to it, Alison felt the line go taut, felt the hard pull on the pole. It almost got away from her.

"I do!" Bracing, she found that it wasn't enough. Whatever was on the other end was strong. "Wow." Holding tight, she was being dragged down the remainder of the bank. "This one's putting up a fight." Unease set in even as she gained her feet. She couldn't seem to stop moving. "Luc?"

He was behind her in a second, his arms going around the pole. And her. "Let go. I'll bring him in for you."

She wasn't even aware of the light laugh that escaped. Alison held on harder. "Not on your life."

He heard the excitement in her voice and understood. There was a thrill, being pitted against nature, vying for supremacy. But he also understood that she'd be dragged into the water in another minute. This wasn't a minnow she'd caught, it was something that had the strength to fight for the all-important victory.

Closing his hands around hers, Luc added his strength to Alison's. And tried not to notice that her hair was brushing against his face. Coupled with the light scent she dabbed on every morning, it was making him feel just the slightest bit light-headed. Desire whispered along the fringes of his consciousness. Telling himself he was just having some sort of allergic reaction to the perfume didn't seem to work.

"Pull!" she yelled at him.

"I am!"

Muscles on his biceps hardened. With his arms bracketing her, it was hard for Alison not to notice. Harder for her not to be affected. With effort, she concentrated on the fish and not the man. "Pull harder, we're losing him!"

His body was as stiff as he could make it, holding fast. "No...I don't...think so."

But they were still moving toward inevitable contact with the water. Alison yelped in surprise when she finally felt it along her shins. Everything within her reacted. The snows on the mountains had only recently melted and run off, making the stream close to icy cold.

Luc heard her teeth chatter. "Reel it in," he ordered. "Reel it in!"

"I *am* reeling!" Alison insisted through clenched teeth.

His hands wrapped even more tightly around hers, Luc pulled the pole back as hard as he could. Alison's foot slipped and they both wound up toppling over backward onto the bank with Alison coming down on top of him. Luc let go of the pole to try to cushion her fall and somehow managed to wind up holding her instead. The shock of contact was more pronounced than the cold water had been.

Her body felt soft and was made of pure temptation. Giddy, self-deprecating laughter echoed and swelled, then faded away into the air as their eyes met.

There was no more room for laughter.

It was hard to say who kissed who first. Luc would have liked to think it was mutual, but he might have been the one to set it in motion.

It didn't really matter.

Whichever way it played, he found his lips crushed against hers. And found liquid fire in his veins. He'd seen an oil fire burning once, and this was like that. Wild, bright and giving all the signs of being out of control.

Except that he knew it couldn't be. There was something about her, something that told him she wasn't ready, no matter how sweet her body felt against his, no matter how inviting this kiss was. He would have thought that he wasn't ready, either. Something inside of him made that a contradiction.

But it took two. And he had never forced a woman to do anything. It wouldn't have occurred to him to even try, no matter what was at stake.

Her head was spinning again. She'd hit it against his chin when they came down, but that didn't have anything to do with it. It was spinning because he was kissing her. Because he'd started that strange chain reaction within her that made her entertain lies. Lies like she could actually follow this through to its natural conclusion. Without freezing.

She knew that wasn't possible. Believing that it was had been what had led her into her marriage. She'd learned fast, hadn't she?

Slowly, her heart hammering wildly, Alison drew back, her hands against his chest, her lungs struggling for air. She shook her head, an Olympic swimmer shaking water off after a race. Except she hadn't won. She hadn't even come close.

She fought hard not to let Luc see what was going on inside her. A smile frozen to her lips, she scrambled quickly to her feet.

Looking toward the stream, she saw her pole disappearing under the water. The fish had won. Not that she would have kept it if she'd been the one to win the battle. She'd meant to throw it back all along. There was no way in the world she could have looked down at the fish struggling on the bank and then gone on to eat it. She would have eaten dandelions first.

Carefully she dusted off her hands on her jeans. "Looks like I owe you a pole."

She owed him more than that, he thought. Another man would have tried to cash in on the promise he'd tasted on her lips. Pushed just enough to make it a reality. It had been there, within his grasp. He didn't know all that much about women, but he'd known that.

But he wasn't another man, he was Luc, and he understood fearing to tread over ground that had once been crossed. Her husband had probably soured her badly on the subject of relationships and she didn't want to make the same mistake again. He could respect that. Hell, wasn't he in the same boat?

Maybe not, he amended, looking into her eyes.

"Forget about it. I lost my grip on it, too." And on himself, as well, he added silently. His own pole was lying lax on the ground where he'd dropped it. "Looks like we'll have to starve to death."

She laughed, glad he'd changed the subject. Grateful he hadn't pressed his advantage. Or said things the way Derek had.

You're nothing but a tease, you know that? A heartless bitch-tease. He hadn't understood and she couldn't explain it to him. Hadn't the words in the face of his scorn.

"Oh, I don't think so." Turning, she linked her arm through Luc's and began to lead the way back to his Jeep. "I know this really great place where they make wonderful salads."

He liked it when she smiled. Everything seemed to light up around her. Picking up his pole, he let himself be led. "Really? Tell me more."

She looked a little wide-eyed, he thought, watching her face as they approached the Inuit village. It wasn't hard to guess what was on her mind. People came with preconceived ideas, born of ancient documentaries and old *National Geographic* photographs.

"Not what you expected, is it?"

"No," she confessed. She banked down her embarrassment. There was only a little, anyway. Luc seemed to understand her mistakes. It made them easier to bear. "I'm not sure what I expected."

Maybe she didn't, but he knew. "Probably igloos and other stereotypical trimmings." What there was in place of that was a collection of single- and two-story houses, little more than upgraded shacks. Some even lacked electricity and running water, although things were being done to remedy that. "Don't feel bad. Most people don't take the trouble to learn that the Inuits have moved into the present century. Ike's mother was half-Inuit." And he'd gotten his first education about the proud people and their traditions from his aunt.

Getting out of his Jeep, Alison reached into the back seat for the medical bag Shayne had lent her. "I'm still having trouble wrapping my tongue around that term. Why aren't they Eskimos anymore?"

He resisted the temptation of putting his arm around her shoulders as they walked toward the village. "That was the Native American's name for them. It means Eater-of-fish." His mouth curved. "Would you want to be known as that if you had a choice?"

"I see your point." She shifted the bag from one hand to the other. It was heavier than she thought. "It's very nice of you to bring me here."

"The kids need these inoculations, and getting them to come into town wasn't an option." It was hard enough getting everyone to agree to their coming into the village. "When Paddy broke his leg, I knew Shayne was going to have to postpone coming out here, so I volunteered to bring you. No big deal. I like coming out here. It's peaceful."

She looked around. "It is that." Luc reached for the bag she was struggling with. Instinct had her closing her hand tighter around the handle. "It's okay, I've got it." She thought of Paddy, in pain and biting his tongue not to say choice words around her when they brought him in. "Do the miners have a lot of accidents?"

"Enough to keep Shayne busy." They were on the outskirts of the village now. "C'mon, I'll help you gather the kids together—or do you have something against that, too?"

"No." She pressed her lips together. "I'm sorry. It's just important to me to be independent, that's all."

"Accepting help once in a while doesn't make a person dependent, it makes them smart."

She bit back a retort. Alison knew he was right. "Okay, here." She thrust the bag toward him.

He merely grinned.

They went from house to house. For the most part, they were admitted warmly, if somewhat shyly. The latter, she realized, had to do with her. But since she was with Luc, the residents of the village allowed her to come into their homes.

Inside, she was amazed to see how very like any other home these homes were. She was even more amazed how highly regarded Luc was among these people. The children flocked to him.

She learned on the way over that there'd been an outbreak of measles just before she'd arrived in Hades. Shayne had used that to finally convince the elders to allow their children to be inoculated. After much hemming and hawing, a date had been set aside. Paddy's broken leg had proven unfortunate for more than Paddy until Luc had volunteered to bring her to the village.

Initially Luc served as an interpreter and go-between, but pretty soon Alison became comfortable with the situation. He had to admire the way she dealt with the children, even the ones who didn't understand her because their parents had insisted that they speak only the "old language." While they couldn't understand the words, the children could understand the look in her eyes. There wasn't even a need for him to translate.

The language sounded incongruous, coming from his lips. The first time he spoke it, Alison paused, looking at him with amazement. It was hard associating him with the man who had lost his memory only weeks earlier. "You speak the language?"

"I grew up here, remember?" He picked up the little boy and said a few words to chase away the fear he saw in the dark eyes before setting him down again.

"Yes, but that doesn't mean you'd know the language. A lot of people don't take the trouble to learn the language of the people around them if their parents don't."

His mother was Swedish, his father French, his aunt half-Inuit and one of his closest friends at the time spoke fluent Russian. There had been a mixture of foreign languages floating in and out of his house while he was growing up.

He shrugged. "Never gave it much thought. The best guy on our baseball team when Ike, Shayne and I were growing up was Noe, an Eskimo. They were called Eskimos back then," he added with an amused smile. His hands on the boy's shoulders to offer silent support, he watched as Alison quickly inoculated the child. The boy's younger sister watched, her eyes as huge as saucers. "You're pretty handy with that."

"I don't see the need to add pain to their fears." She prepared another syringe.

"Your turn, little one," he murmured in Inuit. The little girl shut her eyes and turned her face into his leg, holding on tight.

Alison moved as quickly as she was able. "There, done."

That was the last of them, he thought as she gathered her things together. This was the last house. "Well, Clara Barton, I think you can go home now. Your work here is done."

She closed the medical bag, offering a smile to the

children's mother. Feeling inept that she couldn't say anything to the woman that she would understand. "Tell her—"

"To watch for any signs of fever, yes, I know." He had repeated it, or heard her say it, to every parent.

She waited until they were outside the house before asking, "Clara Barton?"

He took the case from her, but thought better of offering her his arm. He noticed that several of the children who'd been inoculated either came out or were at their windows, watching them leave the village. "The nurse who founded the American Red Cross."

"I know who she is. I just didn't—" She was doing it again, she thought. Alison bit her lip, hoping he took no offense. It was just that she didn't expect someone who lived out here to be well-read. "Sorry."

He took no offense. "You've got to get over the notion that just because the sun does strange things up in this part of the world that it fries our brains, as well. Have you taken a look at Shayne's library?" Opening the Jeep door, he placed the bag in the back.

Alison climbed in on her side. "Yes, but he's a doctor, and well…"

Luc got in behind the wheel and waited until she buckled up before starting the vehicle. "Not only doctors read. Sometimes saloon owners, slash, general store owners, slash, businessmen read, too."

"I'm sorry, slash, really." She grinned, shaking her head at her own actions. "What is it about you that has me tripping over my tongue?"

He glanced at her before turning the Jeep toward Hades. "The feeling's mutual, Alison. The feeling surely is mutual."

* * *

"Wait, there's something I want you to have. I mean, it's something you're going to need if we're to do this right."

Alison turned around, curious. About to walk into Shayne's house after Luc had brought her home, she'd already said goodbye to him.

There was a wedding band in the palm of his hand, its Florentine workmanship long since rubbed away by time and wear, but she could still see traces of it where the light hit it.

For a second, her heart came to a complete stop. Alison raised her eyes to his.

"It was my mother's. And her mother's before that." Holding it out to her had suddenly made him feel tongue-tied, awkward. He'd kept it in his pocket all afternoon, just the way he had when he'd intended to give it to Janice. He had no idea why he'd held back now. It wasn't as if giving her the ring actually meant anything. "My father slipped it on her hand and said the words that bound him to her forever."

"Your father was a minister?"

He grinned. "No. But it was the middle of winter and the town was snowed in. There was no way to get to a minister and my father didn't think he could hold out any longer. But he didn't want my mother to feel as if they were living in sin, either, so they married each other. You can do that in extreme cases," he told her when she lifted a skeptical brow. "It's in the Bible somewhere." He looked at the ring. "She wore this till the day she died. I figured you might need it to pull off the charade."

He noticed that Alison's hand trembled as she held it out to him. He slipped the ring on slowly, his eyes on hers. "There, I now pronounce us make-believe husband and wife."

Alison stared at the ring, remembering other words, vows that turned out to be just as hollow, just as make-believe. "I'll see if I can get used to it by Monday," she mumbled, darting inside.

Luc stood looking at the shut door for a long moment before he finally turned and walked back to his vehicle. He had no idea what to make of the look he'd seen in her eyes.

"So, are you nervous?" Alison whispered the question to Luc as they stood before his house, waiting for his friends to join them.

She'd taken her first tour of his home yesterday after leaving the clinic, trying to orient herself so that she knew where everything was. As far as houses went, it wasn't a very large one, but then she'd come to see that Luc required very little and this suited his needs just fine. Standing on a plot of land his father had left him, not far from the general store, it was a single story, with a wide, friendly kitchen and two bedrooms.

That was the hurdle that was making her nervous, though she tried not to show it.

He kept his eyes on the approaching couple.

"Nothing to be nervous about. He's an old friend. So is she."

Understatements, huge understatements, he thought. Jacob wasn't just an old friend, he was a friend he had lied to. And Janice had never been a friend, she had been an obsession, a feast for a fantasy, and he had loved her as much as a man could. Blindly.

And now they both were walking toward him, arm in arm. Was he ready to live out his lie?

Chapter Twelve

Alison sat across the table from Janice, pretending to eat, trying to keep her thoughts from registering on her face.

She'd taken an instant dislike to Janice.

Admittedly, it wasn't very fair of her. Under ordinary circumstances, she wasn't the type to make snap judgments. But over the last three weeks, busy though she'd been, the bond that had formed between her and Luc in the alley in Seattle had strengthened. She'd gotten to genuinely like Luc. And to respect him for what he was and what he was trying to do within the community.

There was no doubt that he was a selfless man rather than a selfish one. It was a rare quality in a person. She didn't like seeing that kind of person hurt.

Ike had told her in passing that it was precisely that rare quality that had pushed Janice away from Luc and into the arms of another man. A man who wanted to do great things and make huge piles of money while he was at it. A man who was going places while Luc was content to remain at home.

Her eyes slanted toward Jacob, before looking back at her plate. Sensing that he was looking her way, she forced herself to smile.

She couldn't fault Jacob for a trait that was alive and well within the older of her two older brothers. There was nothing wrong with drive and ambition; she'd always admired it herself. But what she could fault Jacob for was hurting Luc.

Funny how protective she'd gotten of a man who looked as if protecting was the last thing in the world he needed.

But then, she wasn't alone in that feeling. Otherwise, why would the people in the town have all conspired to play along with this charade? It was to help someone they liked save face. The very fact was a credit to the kind of man Luc was.

Picking up her glass of wine, wine that Jacob and Janice had brought with them as a gift from Los Angeles, Alison took a sip and dwelled on what the townspeople were doing for Luc.

A person could do a lot worse than live .in a place like this. She was beginning to see why Luc had such an affinity for Hades.

The tension of maintaining the pretense while appearing at ease danced over her. It had been far from a walk in the park. She was feeling her way around blindly, trying to remember to answer to "Suzanne" and to keep all the details she and Luc had created straight in her mind.

This last hour she'd done her best to act the genial hostess, a role that ill suited her, given how poorly she knew her way around a kitchen. Whatever success she'd had she attributed to pretending to be Lily, with a pinch or two of Sydney thrown in. Lily was never at a loss when it came to throwing a party, no matter how large or small. She would have found a way to materialize candles and tablecloths for everyone to go along with the five fishes and two loaves of bread that had fed the masses during the Sermon on the Mount. Sydney would have provided the homey warmth.

But warmth was a difficult thing to force whenever she looked at Janice. The woman was striking, no doubt about it. She was a willowy blonde with a killer figure, long, straight hair and eyes the color of a blue jay's wings spread in flight.

And she had broken Luc's heart.

Still listening to the three other people at the table relive past episodes, Alison excused herself and began gathering the plates, all empty save hers.

She caught the pointed look Jacob gave his wife. Caught, too, that Janice looked away.

"Need help?" Jacob finally asked.

She shook her head. "I'm just putting them in the sink for now."

Luc picked up the plates on his side of the table and brought them in for her. Though he seemed to be enjoying the company of his friends and catching up with them, he looked slightly preoccupied. It was probably because the pretense was weighing heavily on his mind.

He made her think of someone who would have pledged his honor to Arthur at the Round Table.

"The prime rib was excellent," Jacob enthused as they all retired from the table and took the five short steps into the rustic-looking living room. "I've eaten in some of the finest restaurants in this country and I can honestly say I've never had any better.''

For a second she grappled with accepting the compliment, but they were dealing with enough fabrication already. She didn't want to compound it even more. Not that there was the danger of Janice asking her for the recipe. The woman looked even less inclined to find her way around a kitchen than she was.

"Then the compliment should go to Luc," Alison told him. She deliberately wove her arm through Luc's, getting a kick out of the mild surprise that rose in his eyes. "Luc made the meal. I was just the kitchen help."

"Why is it we can't find help like that, Janice?" Jacob joked. Taking a seat on the sofa, he moved to one side, making room for his wife.

She chose to sit down on the love seat instead. She also chose to ignore the good-humored question. Janice watched as the other couple sat down beside Jacob. With exaggerated movements, she laced and folded her hands together, her attention on Alison.

"So you're a nurse?" Janice asked. Alison nodded, but before she could say anything, Janice's eyes had shifted to Luc. "You never mentioned Suzanne was a nurse."

He found it difficult to think of the woman beside him as anything else than Alison. Not after he'd just spent the last three weeks referring to her by that name.

Thinking of her by that name.

"The subject never came up," Jacob told his wife, coming to his friend's rescue.

Making himself comfortable by loosening his belt, he raised the glass he'd brought over with him from the dining room, in a toast to Luc. Alison saw the look of barely veiled annoyance pass over Janice's face. She didn't know if it was because of the toast Jacob was about to propose, or the belt he had unnotched. Probably both.

"Looks like you've done really well for yourself." His eyes swept over Alison. "Luc doesn't talk a lot, so I had to pump Shayne for information on the way over here." Jacob looked at his old friend. "Shayne said you own the general store now and are thinking of going in on the theater."

Luc shrugged vaguely. He didn't care for discussing business matters, especially when things weren't solidified. "Thought it might not be a bad idea. Wayne's strapped for cash."

Jacob laughed, taking another sip. "Wayne Hardgrove." He shook his head, remembering things as they had once been. "Never thought he'd stick around. Now you, you I knew always would." It somehow figured that Luc would come to the other man's rescue, whether financial or otherwise. That was the kind of person he was. "Your husband's the stablest man I ever met," he confided to Alison. "He likes something, he sticks by it come hell or high water."

If it seemed like praise to Jacob when he said it, it wasn't to his wife. Janice toyed with her glass. The contents didn't hold her attention the way Luc could. She began to think of opportunities lost and the road not taken. Why was it that the other side of the fence always seemed so much more tempting?

"Don't you sometimes regret staying here?" she prodded, leaning forward over the massive coffee table.

It sounded to Alison like the tail end of an ongoing debate they'd carried on not all that long ago. "Why should he regret it?" she interjected. "He's got good friends and the good feeling of building up a place he's always loved. All the big cities of the world were once nothing more than a collection of a few houses.''

The look in Janice's eyes was incredulous. Though she had gone on to someone else, she hadn't made her peace with the fact that Luc had, too. That he had stung her pride more than a little, even though she knew it was being unreasonable. ''Are you telling me you think Hades is going to be a big city?''

Alison couldn't tell if the other woman was ridiculing her, or just being argumentative. ''No, I'm saying that underneath it all, the foundation that goes into making a place is pretty similar.'' Her defensiveness rose higher. She didn't care what the woman thought of her, but she resented that she was looking down her nose at Luc and the path he'd chosen to take. ''And there's nothing wrong in putting your faith and your time into a place rather than a thing.''

Jacob appeared mildly amused. ''By thing I take it you mean a company?''

She hadn't meant to insult him. She had a tendency to get carried away and Luc wasn't saying anything in his own defense. Because she didn't want to make the situation uncomfortable, Alison retreated slightly. ''I'm sorry, I didn't mean for it to sound as if I'm denigrating what you've done—''

Jacob held up a hand to stop the apology before it got rolling. ''No offense taken. Like I said, Luc's done very well for himself.'' He avoided looking at Janice, knowing this would rankle her. But it was the truth. ''And maybe I envy him a little.''

''Envy?'' Janice echoed, stunned. ''In heaven's name, why?''

Janice had never been one to see the beauty in simplicity. But then, Jacob hadn't loved her for that. He loved her for her support, her ambition, her enthusiasm. For the most part, he needed someone like that at his side. But right now he was just a little tired of his world and its demands.

"Because there's no treadmill running at top speed under Luc's feet, no threat of being caught by that same treadmill and dragged through the machinery." Realizing that he sounded as if he was getting on a soapbox, Jacob stopped himself and laughed. "Don't get me wrong, I wouldn't come here to live and give everything up I've worked for. It's just that, sometimes…"

Luc understood. "You need a place to get away. To hear yourself think."

Jacob inclined his head. "You always did know me better than I knew myself."

Luc glanced at Janice and remembered the hurt. The hurt that time had muted and placed under glass. "No, not always."

They talked for a while longer. Then, at Jacob's insistence, since the movie theater was a new addition and hadn't been in Hades while he'd lived in the town, they went to see the building. Once there, because the timing was right, they decided to take in the movie.

By the time they returned home, the hour was late and jet lag was catching up to them. They had flown here from New York.

Outside, a touch of twilight was sneaking in, determined to make an appearance before dawn came to chase it away. The night would be less than a few hours long.

Jacob shrugged out of the jacket he'd worn all evening, making himself comfortable. "I think we'd better call it a night.'' He looked at his wife. "I feel tired enough to actually sleep for a change.''

Janice looked through her purse, producing the small bottle of pills she made sure she carried with her on trips. "Just take one of these, honey.''

Alison noticed the prescription label. It was for sleeping pills. The dosage was a large one. How long had Jacob been taking those, she wondered.

"You're having trouble sleeping?'' Luc asked.

"Too much on my mind.'' Jacob didn't feel like going into details at this hour. Maybe tomorrow, when they were alone. Luc had always been easy to talk to. "Business doesn't run itself.''

Saying something to the effect that maybe it was time Jacob delegated a little of his responsibilities, Luc showed Jacob and Janice to their room.

He then moved toward his own room, a sense of wonder filling him. Beneath the trappings, Jacob hadn't really changed all that much; he was still Jacob. And beneath her trappings, Luc discovered, Janice was a woman he really hadn't known at all. Seeing her had momentarily stirred up old feelings. But listening to her this evening had quickly squelched them.

Things always did turn out for the best, he mused. He was lucky that Janice had recognized how incompatible they actually were and had gone after someone who was far more in tune to her own wants and needs. Had Luc and Janice gotten married, they would have made each other miserable within a month.

The door to his bedroom was partially open. He pushed it open all the way, knocking first. Alison swung around to look at him. She was wearing pajamas one size too large for her. He'd never seen anything so hopelessly sexy in his life.

She told herself that she was being stupid, that there was no reason to feel this way. As if she was about to walk over a floor carpeted with spiders. This was Luc, after all, and he hadn't given her any reason not to trust him. But she couldn't seem to bank down the feeling.

"Um…we never discussed—accommodations." Trying not to sound utterly adolescent, Alison nodded toward the bed.

Unbuttoning his shirt, he pulled the ends out of his jeans, then shed it. "Nothing to discuss. I figured you'd get the bed, I'd get the floor." Crossing to the closet, he took out the extra comforter and tossed it beside the four-poster.

She looked away as he pulled his belt out of the loops. He debated putting on the pajama bottoms he slept in, then decided that she would feel better if he just stayed in his jeans.

Not hearing anything, she ventured a look and saw that he had stopped undressing. Because he'd offered to do the gallant thing without any fanfare or any request on her part, Alison felt compelled to make her own counteroffer. This was, after all, his room. "The bed's large enough for two."

The innocent observation made him grin. "That was the thought my father was going with when he bought it for himself and my mother."

He probably thought she was some virginal novice. *Well, for all intents and purposes, aren't you?*

Alison tried again. "What I mean is that we're both adults and there's no reason we can't be adult about sharing a bed." She gestured toward it, nerves making her sound impatient. "You take one side, I'll take the other." Her eyes met his with stony resolve. "Nothing has to happen."

No, nothing *has* to, he thought, but there was a little uneasiness that it might. That was what she was thinking. He could sense it even if there hadn't been that fleeting look in her eyes when he'd walked in.

"All right." He gathered up the comforter and tossed it on top of the bed. She might feel better if they each had their own blanket. "But just remember this is your idea." He pretended to scrutinize her closely. "You're not planning to have your way with me, are you?"

"No, not planning on it." Despite her feelings, he'd managed to coax a smile out of her.

"All right then, let's get some sleep." He lay down on the bed and, wrapping the comforter around himself, he shut his eyes.

Like someone testing the waters to see if they were too cold, Alison slowly slipped into the bed beside him. The fact that they had separate comforters didn't help. He was a heartbeat away from her and she was lying right there next to him, listening to him breathe. Each breath seemed to vibrate inside her chest.

It had been two years since she'd shared a bed with a man. And back then, toward the end, it had been a nest of hostility and recriminations.

She tried to sleep.

She couldn't.

"Luc?"

"Hmm?" He sounded as if he was more than half-asleep.

"What did you ever see in Janice?"

The question roused him. He turned on his side to give her a quizzical look. His face was only a few inches away from hers. She could feel his breath on her cheek when he exhaled. Something tightened sharply in the pit of her stomach.

And in her loins.

She could feel her pulse accelerating.

Nervous, she ran the tip of her tongue along her bottom lip before biting it. "I mean, other than the obvious. I mean, she is beautiful and all that, but she seems so, I don't know, mercenary." Her voice was accelerating with each word. "Like everything has to be about money, and that's not what everything should be about. It should be about feelings and—"

She was babbling and she knew it, but there was this sudden need for words, for rhetoric to fill up the space between them. To be packed in so tightly that he didn't hear how loud her heart was pounding. That he didn't notice that she wanted his arms around her. His lips on hers.

Raising himself up on his elbow, Luc peered into her face. And felt those same needs slamming into him again, this time with the force of a football player plowing into the opposition. "Alison?"

He seemed to be directly over her. "Yes?" She nearly coughed out the word, her throat was so dry.

"Do you think you could stop talking for maybe just a second?"

Her breath caught in her throat. "Why?" she asked hoarsely. "Because you want to sleep?"

The smile that curved his mouth was slow and sensual as his eyes held hers. "Not exactly."

And then his smile was on her lips, passed there by touch. Luc slipped his hand between her hair and the pillow, his fingers tangling in the long curly strands as he cupped the back of her head.

He kissed her, kissed her because at this moment in his life, there was absolutely nothing else he wanted to do but that.

Like a match striking the side of a tinderbox, it lit the fire within him.

Signals quickened inside Alison, heating her. Melting her. Sensations, tantalizing and delicious, rushed out to greet her. Surprise her. Without thinking, she wrapped her arms around his neck, surrendering herself to the kiss and to the wild feelings it generated.

And then, just as quickly, the feelings receded into the shadows as unsummoned memories intruded, commandeering her mind. Freezing her body.

She began to tremble.

He knew the difference. He'd felt anticipation tremble within him. Cause the woman he was with to tremble. This was not the same.

Concerned, he drew away from her. "Alison, what's wrong?" He saw that same terrified look in her eyes. She moved her head from side to side, struggling to hold back the tears. "Nothing."

He didn't understand what was happening. He hadn't forced himself on her. But then, there were different definitions of the word, he supposed. Maybe in her mind he had forced something.

He didn't want her afraid of him. Didn't want her thinking she was in any danger. Falling back to his side, he stared up at the ceiling. "That got a little out of hand."

Braced to hear him revile her, there was nothing but shock when he didn't. She could say nothing, plead nothing. Any words would only make things worse. Pressing her lips together, she turned away before he could see the tears in her eyes.

Further apologies would only make things worse, he

thought, so instead he turned away from her and willed himself to fall asleep. Maybe they could sort things out in the morning.

A noise wedged itself into his dream. The sound of an animal, hurt, keening.

No, not keening and not an animal…

Trying to unravel the mystery nudged him out of the realm of sleep into wakefulness. His eyes still shut, he listened. Was that the wind?

No, he changed his mind. The wind didn't weep. Forgetting that he wasn't alone in the room, he turned to face the middle of the bed. The moment he did, he remembered.

But there was no body to bump into. The bed was empty, the place beside him, when he felt it, cold.

He sat up and looked around.

Though it had to be around one, dawn was already staking a claim to the day, urging the crickets outside to end their symphony and go home.

There was someone sitting on the window seat. Alison. Her head was on her knees, with her arms wrapped around them as if she was trying to make herself small. Make herself disappear.

That's what the sound was. She was crying.

Watching her, Luc was torn between giving Alison her privacy and giving her comfort. The struggle was a short one. Unable to see her suffering like this, for whatever the reason, Luc got up and crossed to her.

She didn't even seem to hear him approach. Very gently he laid his hand on her hair and stroked it. "Alison?"

She jerked as if he'd used a hot poker, but didn't raise her head. She couldn't. "Go away. I can't talk to you right now."

"Nobody's asking you to talk." Moved, wanting only to ease whatever it was that hurt her so, Luc began to take her into his arms.

Resisting, she bunched her hands against his chest and tried to push him away. The tearstains on her face caught him off guard and wrenched his heart.

"I said go away, I don't want you to see me like this." He probably thought she was crazy. Maybe she was. Alison wasn't even sure why she was crying; she just knew she couldn't help it.

But he wouldn't be pushed away. Instead he gathered her to him on his lap and sat down on the window seat. "Shh," he whispered against her hair, "you won't even know I'm here."

Slowly, like a summer wave along the beach, his soothing tone penetrated her agitated state. Alison stopped resisting and allowed the comfort in. "I feel so stupid...."

"We all do," he told her quietly, "at one time or another."

He was being so understanding, it made her feel guilty and more conflicted than she ever had with Derek. Because Derek had called her names, had belittled her when the smattering of patience he'd had had disappeared. In her heart, she couldn't even blame Derek. How could she? He'd thought he was getting a wife.

"I'm sorry, Luc."

He knew she was, though he didn't completely understand what was going on or what torment she was putting herself through, only that she was sorry that somehow it had extended enough to touch him.

"Shh, nothing to be sorry for. Nothing at all." He

continued holding her, rocking slightly, until she fell asleep in his arms.

Leaning his cheek against her hair, he decided that there were worse ways to spend a night.

Chapter Thirteen

There was no time for Alison to talk to Luc and apologize.

The next two days were a flurry of activity, even by normal standards, let alone the ones she had come to expect here in Hades. Though Shayne had made the offer to give her a little time off, she'd declined, feeling it safer all around if she were working. There was less of a chance of a misstep on her part with Jacob and Janice.

And less of a chance to do the same with Luc.

She was secretly grateful for the accelerated pace that work and playing hostess created because as well as any tabled apology to Luc, it also put off any questions he might have had.

There was no doubt in her mind that Luc was a wonderful man. But she'd thought the same once of Derek. Wonderful lost its luster when confronted with the same frustrating situation day in, day out. She couldn't really blame her ex. It was her fault.

There was a line in her head, a line she couldn't cross, no matter how much she wanted to. She froze at that line, unable to reach out, unable to be reached.

And if ever she'd wanted to be reached, it was now....

There was no point in dwelling on it, Alison told herself as she parked the Jeep in front of the Salty. She was late meeting everyone as it was. Besides, going over the situation again wouldn't change anything. All it would do would make her feel guiltier. She was what she was and there was no making a passionate woman out of one whose blood turned cold at the slightest sign of intimacy.

Still sitting in the Jeep, Alison pressed her lips together. She had no business responding to Luc, no business in allowing him to think, even for a second, that there could be anything between them. Because even though she was stirred, she knew what would happen. Exactly what had happened two nights ago. Nothing. She went so far and no further.

It was a fact of life. Her life.

You have a party to go to, for God's sake—smile.

She knew that half the people in Hades were probably in the Salty. If she came in looking as if she'd just attended two funerals in a row, word was going to spread faster than fire over dried prairie grass. People would start asking her what was wrong. They were like that here—eager to listen, eager to help.

Determined to behave like the blissful newlywed Luc deserved, she got out of the vehicle and walked over to the Salty's front door. Taking a deep breath, she pushed open the door and was immediately absorbed.

There was no other way to describe it. The Salty opened both its arms to her the instant she crossed the threshold, and welcomed her with a warm embrace. Just the way it had the first time she'd been here. There was something about the bright, cheery place that sang of camaraderie and comfort.

It was a little, she thought, like coming home after a long, weary day. It wasn't hard for her to see the attraction of the place. It pleased her that it was run by Ike and Luc.

Now all that remained was finding them—and the others.

Scanning the room, Alison saw them instantly. Jacob and Janice were holding court in the center of the room, talking, she assumed, to people they'd once known. The place was literally packed with people. It was easy to forget, standing here in this throng, that Hades was actually very thinly populated.

She looked for her own set of familiar faces. The unease she'd held under wraps only three weeks ago was gone as she glanced around the room. She was getting to know most of these people by sight, thanks to the parade of so-called patients that had gone through Shayne's office to eyeball her on a one-to-one basis.

Predominantly, she admitted to herself, she was looking for Luc.

He found her first. Coming up behind her, he slipped an arm around her waist and kissed the top of her hair. "Hi. I see you made it."

She started, then forced herself to relax. It was, she had to admit, getting easier. "Yes."

He kept his arm around her waist. "I thought this would look more natural to Janice and Jacob, like we were actually married," he whispered against her ear.

Had he noticed that she'd stiffened? Of course he had. There was no way he could have missed it. When would the random touch of a man's hand not set her off like this?

"Good idea," she murmured. "And thanks for leaving the Jeep for me. It was nice getting behind the wheel again." She grinned. "I never thought I'd hear myself say it, but I miss driving."

The din was getting louder. He inclined his head toward her. "It's being forced to do something that takes away from the pleasure."

She looked at him sharply. Was he trying to tell her something? And then she dismissed it as being silly on her part. He was just making a random observation. There was no way he could know about the turn her marriage had taken. He didn't even know she'd been married.

She nodded toward the center table. "They look like they're enjoying themselves." Taking a closer look, she reevaluated her impression. "At least, Jacob does."

Jacob had always been able to have a good time, when he laid aside his goals. "He liked it here well enough," Luc remembered. "But there weren't enough opportunities for him."

She turned her face toward Luc, very much aware that his hand was still around her waist. And that she liked it there.

"But there were for you." It wasn't a question.

He shrugged as he carefully guided her back to the main table. "We were looking for different things."

The comment peaked her interest. "And did you find what you were looking for?"

His eyes swept over her, warming her skin even more than the close quarters did. "I'm getting there."

Before she had a chance to ask where "there" was, Ike came up on her other side and planted a quick, cousinly kiss on her lips. "About time you got here." He pulled up a chair for her.

The others hailed her as she sat down, though she noted that Janice's greeting was a little cool. "I had some things to finish up," Alison explained.

Ike shook his head. "Works you like a slave, doesn't he, darlin'?" Not giving her a chance to come to Shayne's defense, he placed a brandy glass in front of her. It was filled with a bright pink, foamy-looking liquid. "Here, I want you to try this, tell me what you think of it."

It looked tempting. She turned the glass around slowly by its stem. The light overhead shimmered over the surface. "What is it?"

"Something I made up for Marta. I call it Smiles." Ike waved his hand at the room, a collection of regulars mingled in with people who generally did their celebrating at home. The men outnumbered the women seven to one. "Don't get much of a chance to serve it to this crowd. Drink up, tell me what you think. Puts roses in your cheeks."

"And a buzz in your head," Marta added, laughing. With a grin, Ike threw his arm around his wife and pulled her closer to him.

Luc drew his chair closer to Alison's. "You don't have to have that if you don't want to." She probably preferred wine. It was what he'd seen her drinking at the club in Seattle. He reached for the glass. "I can bring you something else."

She stayed his hand. "No, that's okay. I like trying new things."

"Oh, you've got yourself a rare woman, there, boyo," Paddy cackled behind them. He hobbled by, leaning on his crutch and holding tightly to his glass of beer with the other hand.

Feeling as if she'd suddenly become the center of attention, Alison took a tentative sip from the glass. A warm, sunny feeling seemed to pour slowly through her as she felt the liquid spread out through her veins.

It was the same sort of feeling, she thought, she had whenever she caught Luc smiling at her. Her eyes met Ike's. "This is good."

Vindicated, Ike didn't bother hiding his triumph as he looked at his cousin. "Told you she'd like it."

"He's going to be impossible to live with, you realize that," Luc told Alison.

"He already is," Marta countered, tucking her arms around her husband's torso and inclining her head against his shoulder. "Especially since he just found out he's going to be a father."

"But you already are," Alison pointed out.

Marta grinned. "Yes, but this time he actually put down the groundwork himself."

The men at Marta's elbow hooted.

Amid congratulations, everyone took their turn pounding Ike on the back, but Alison noticed that the glance Jacob exchanged with Janice had a solemnity in it that almost hurt to witness. She looked away before either one could realize that she'd noticed it.

Raising her glass high, she was the first to toast the prospective parents, finishing the remainder of her drink.

"Thanks, darlin'," Ike squeezed her shoulder.

Her head was buzzing. Walking into the bedroom, she felt lighter than a scrap of nylon being whisked away by a playful spring breeze.

Smiling, she hugged herself.

"You certainly seem happy tonight."

His voice surrounded her. She turned a little too sharply to look at him. Wobbly, she lost her bearings for a second. The next moment, he was beside her, grabbing her by the arms and holding her.

She closed her eyes and welcomed the feeling.

"I am," she breathed, opening her eyes again. How was it that she'd been running from this, when it felt so wonderful? When he felt so wonderful?

She placed her hands on his arms when he began to release her. "No, don't."

The soft entreaty whispered along his skin, tightening his gut. Playing havoc with everything in between.

He'd spent most of the evening watching her. And wanting her.

There'd been something different about her tonight. She'd seemed happier, freer. The tension he'd seen along her brow was gone. Even now, her laughter still felt as if it was trapped within his chest, teasing his heart.

Just like her body, so tantalizingly close, was teasing his.

A man knew his limits and he was swiftly approaching his. He tried to loosen his hold on her again. "Alison, I think for your own good—"

Her hands remained where they were. She was standing very close to the edge now, and the fear hadn't come yet. She could feel her heart all but leaping for joy inside her.

Her eyes held his. She slipped her arms around his neck. "Maybe I don't want to think about my own good right now. Maybe I don't want to think at all."

Did she even have a clue what she was doing to him? He doubted it. "I'm only human, Alison."

"I know." Standing on her toes, she brought her

mouth very close to his. So close that the kiss was there between them before it touched his mouth.

It took everything he had to try to hold her off and himself in check. He figured this qualified him for a spot beside Galahad at Arthur's Round Table. Either that, or a Purple Heart for valor above and beyond the call. "You don't know what you're doing."

"Maybe I do." Feeling wonderful, feeling freer than she had in years, Alison made her affirmation by pressing a small, nerve-scrambling kiss to his neck.

Luc's eyes fluttered shut as he absorbed the sensation. It shot through his body like an urgent alarm. "Is this some sort of a test?" he said with effort as her lips moved along his throat, slowly undoing him. His arms involuntarily tightened around her. "Because if it is, I don't know what I'm supposed to do to pass."

She drew her head back. Her eyes were wide when they looked at him. Wide and clear. "Take me away from everything. From all these things inside my head."

Before he could protest, for her sake because it definitely wasn't for his, she sealed her mouth to his. And sealed their fate.

Passion flared instantly, like kerosene suddenly thrown on smoldering flames, making them burst into sheets of fire. That's how her body felt. Like it had burst into flame. And burned brightly.

She wanted him. Desperately. And wanted him to want her.

Unable to help himself, praying that there would be forgiveness somewhere in the night, Luc gave up the fight and gave in to her.

And to himself.

Over and over again, he kissed her. Kissed her eyes, her lips, her face, the curve of her neck, the hollow of her throat. Kissed the creamy, delicate shoulders beneath the blouse he almost ripped from her in his attempt to draw the material away.

A button was lost in the skirmish.

"Sorry," he breathed.

Her head spinning, Alison ignored the rest of the buttons and quickly pulled her blouse up, over her head, throwing it on the floor. "I know how to sew."

With that, she yanked both sides of his shirt apart, sending more buttons flying after the first. The remaining slid from their holes on contact. Breathing hard, she pulled the material down his shoulders.

"Good thing," he murmured.

Curtailing eagerness at every turn, he worked his way along her chin, grazing it with his teeth. When she moaned, he thought his own knees would buckle. How could something so delicate reduce him to such a mass of wants and desires so quickly? How could it take a strong, strapping man in his prime and turn him into something that bore a startling resemblance to a bowl of hot oatmeal?

It didn't matter how. What mattered was that she had. Easily.

Because he wanted to give her every opportunity to pull back, even if the price would be his own self-destruction, Luc forced himself to slow down. And thus to tantalize and tease them both beyond endurance by doing so.

With his forefinger, he caught the inside of her jeans, slowly passing the tip of his finger along the sensitive skin of her quivering belly. He could feel his own breathing growing shallow, speeding up until the sound of it matched the tempo he heard coming from her. Slowly, his eyes on hers, he flipped the metallic button out of the hole and then, even more slowly, slid the zipper down to its source. The look in her eyes excited him, urged him on.

She tightened her fingers on his triceps as he slipped both hands inside her jeans, coaxing them from her hips, inch by torturous inch.

A flare went up, searing through the hot passion that was enveloping her. A sliver of icy panic she fought to beat back.

He could feel it, feel the alarm she was struggling to overcome. Concern took precedence over desire. "Alison? What is it?"

"Nothing." She pressed her lips to his. "Nothing." She would outrace it, she would. This one time she wouldn't allow it to ruin things.

The kiss deepened. The wild spinning in her head returned and she clung to it, concentrating on it, focusing on Luc, and not on the specter of fear that stood just outside the perimeter of her consciousness, searching for a crack to wedge through.

She was like a woman possessed, he thought. His realm of experience was not nearly as broad as his cousin's and he had never had a woman do these kinds of things to him, create such sensations within him. He hardly knew himself. There was tenderness, but it was framed in passion the likes of which he could barely control.

Kicking away his own jeans, Luc took her to his bed, laying her down and enveloping her in his arms. In his world.

Wildly she struggled to draw this bit of happiness to her before all her castles in the sky came crashing down. Before the fear she had lived with all these years, fanned by a dark memory, rose up to destroy everything and freeze her.

"Make love with me, Luc," she breathed, her chest brushing against his, enflaming him.

He paused, gathering what was left of his senses. Brushing aside the damp hair that had plastered itself against her forehead, he looked down at her face. Very lightly his fingers ran along her cheek. He didn't see fear in her eyes, but was it still hovering somewhere, waiting for her, waiting for a weak moment? He wanted this to be as wondrous for her as it was for him. Otherwise it wasn't any good.

A smile lifted the corners of his mouth. "I thought that's what I was doing."

She wasn't saying it right again, but this was no time to search for the right words. "I mean, take me, now."

He wanted to. Needed to, but there was pleasure in prolonging the journey, in making her feel desirable, precious, and he meant to give her that.

His mouth beside her temple, he whispered, "Slowly, Alison, slowly," and drove her utterly insane.

Demands drummed through her, shrieking for release. Wanting, just this once, to reach their peak and burst. She arched against him, her body pleading her case more urgently, more eloquently, than her words ever could.

Still he held to his silent promise to give her more, making love to her with every fiber of his being. Touching gently, caressing not fondling, and all the while, worshiping her and this heretofore undiscovered sensation that he'd now laid claim to.

Until he couldn't resist the siren song any longer.

He'd reduced her to a mindless puddle of quivering needs and responses. There was nothing but haze around her. Haze and his wondrous face. She saw it above her now as she felt his body draw slowly over hers. Her heart quickened, feeling the edginess of fear approaching. Without a word, she opened for him, arched toward him. Ready, wanting. Hopeful.

She bit her lip when he came to her, struggled against the pressure she felt as he filled her. Her nails dug into his shoulders and her muffled cry was swallowed up within his mouth. And then, the fear that had been encroaching vanished as she began to move with him. Move urgently toward the final pleasure.

When it came, she bit her lip to keep from crying out her exhalation. She'd never reached this peak before, never felt a climax shudder through her body, bringing with it a taste of paradise. Euphoria blanketed her.

Heart slamming against her ribs, breath depleted, she fell back, exhausted. Alison didn't even realize that her eyes were squeezed shut until she opened them again. And looked up at his face.

She had no idea what she expected to see there. Pity? Triumph? Annoyance? She wasn't sure. All she knew was that she couldn't read his expression, but his eyes were kind.

Luc stroked back her hair again, then lightly kissed her lips. "Does that qualify?"

She didn't understand. "Qualify?"

"As making love." Maybe she didn't remember. "In the middle of it, you asked me to make love with you and I just wanted to make sure everything met with your satisfaction." He pressed a kiss to her forehead. And felt her withdraw. "Did it?"

She turned her face into the pillow. "Don't make fun of me."

Very gently he coaxed her back to look at him. "Oh,

lady, after what just happened, there's no way I have the strength to make fun of you.''

A flicker of hope, of pride, came. It was silly, and yet it wouldn't leave her. ''Then it was all right?''

Didn't she know? Couldn't she feel what had just happened? ''It was 'all right' only if you have a very, very limited vocabulary.'' He kissed her cheek, but she didn't turn toward him. Whatever it was that held her in its grip was still there. And vying for possession of her again. The debate was short-lived. ''I make it a practice never to pry, Alison, but if you want to talk to me...'' He let his voice trail off, letting her fill in whatever needed to be filled.

Caution and suspicion were in her eyes. ''About?''

He wished he had Ike's gift for phrasing things. But he hadn't, and he did the best he could, armed only with good intentions and his own desire to make her feel better. ''About whatever it is that makes you so afraid every time I touch you.''

Why did he have to ruin things by asking questions? She'd tried her very best to be what he wanted her to be. ''I wasn't afraid just then.''

That wasn't entirely true, but he let her have the lie. And even so, she'd needed a crutch to be with him like this. ''Only because you'd had a drink or two.'' The look in her eyes told him that he'd struck a nerve. ''It let you put aside whatever it is that's bothering you, but that's not a permanent solution.''

She wished he'd stop. ''There is no permanent solution.''

He moved off her and gathered her to him. He could feel her stiffening. Resisting what he was saying. ''Talking it out is a start. My mother used to say that if something was bothering you and you didn't let it out, it only got bigger and bigger—until it was bigger than you.'' Her silence echoed between them. ''Is that what happened, Alison? Did it get bigger than you?''

She sighed, feeling tears gathering in her throat. ''Maybe.''

''Derek?'' he guessed.

She looked at him in surprise. ''How did you know about Derek?''

''Kevin told me.'' He saw the look that came into her eyes. ''Don't blame him. That last night we were there, I asked if you were leaving anyone behind. He told me about your divorce.''

Alison shook her head. ''No, it's not Derek. Derek just got caught in the cross fire.''

Luc heard more than she was saying. ''But he didn't help.''

Alison pressed her lips together, not wanting to say any more. Feeling she owed him at least something of an explanation. ''No, he didn't help. To be fair, I never told him, either. I thought that I could get over it on my own. Outgrow it.''

He rose on his elbow, his eyes intent on her face. ''What 'it'? Alison?'' He saw the resistance grow. ''I'm not prying, I want to help.''

She wanted to tell him, really wanted to. But the words refused to come out. They'd been locked inside for so long. The memory had been locked inside and if she opened it, the shame would return. The shame she swore she would never allow to take possession of her.

''You can help by not asking me.'' Gathering the comforter to her, she wrapped it around her body and got up. ''I'm going to get ready for bed.''

Frustrated, he watched her disappear into the bathroom. He couldn't force her to tell him, so for now he'd let her retreat. But he meant to get to the bottom of whatever it was that was haunting her.

And soon.

Chapter Fourteen

When he woke up the next morning, Alison was just coming out of the bathroom. Freshly showered with the smell of herbal soap about her, she was dressed and ready to leave.

She was going to go without saying a single word to him. The thought saddened and angered him at the same time. He didn't usually get angry.

"Alison?" He heard her sharp intake of breath, as if he'd caught her off guard.

She'd hoped to leave before Luc was awake, wanting to avoid him and any possible scene. It was the way she and Derek had lived out the last weeks of their marriage—avoiding one another.

Without turning in his direction, she indicated the door. "I was just on my way out."

"I kind of figured that out on my own." He paused, waiting for her to say something, to turn around. When she didn't, he got out of bed and crossed to her. Tension took up three quarters of the bedroom. "We can't go outside this room like this."

Forced to look at him, she raised her head and met his eyes. "Don't worry, I'll still go on pretending that I'm your wife."

It took a great deal of self-control for him not to grab her arms and shake sense into her head. He had no idea what had come over him. He wasn't a physical man, not in that way. But last night had broken all the rules.

"Damn it, I don't care about what you're pretending. I care about what's going on inside your head." He raked his hand through his hair, struggling to maintain control, searching for an anchor. "Look, Alison, if I took advantage of you last night in any way..."

She stared at him, her voice deadly calm. He hadn't a clue what was in her mind. "You think you took advantage of me?"

He shrugged, helpless. Damning himself for his own weakness. "Well, you did have a few Smiles in you by the time we came home."

A jagged sigh escaped her lips. "If you thought that I was drunk, why didn't you stop?"

"Not drunk, just light-headed." And so damn tempting, a saint couldn't have turned away. "And I didn't stop because I couldn't. I tried, but you were so beautiful and so passionate—"

You were just so pretty, Alison. The memory stabbed at her, she felt as if she'd received a physical wound. "So it's my fault."

He stared at her. "Nobody used the word *fault.*"

Her eyes were accusing as she raised them to his. "But that's what you meant."

He'd always had infinite patience; why didn't he have

any now? "Damn it, stop putting words into my mouth, Alison."

She could hear the anger, reined in, but there nonetheless. Like Derek right after the beginning. Derek, who'd demanded his connubial rights. An urgency to flee came over her. She moved around Luc to the door. "If you'll excuse me, I have to get to work."

He caught her wrist, turning her around. There was accusation in her eyes. Angry with himself for what he was doing, and with her for bringing out emotion he'd never known existed, he let her hand go. But he still stood blocking the door.

He had no idea what to say, how to begin. So he didn't. "We have a picnic to go to this afternoon."

She nodded curtly. "You know where to find me."

"That's just it," he said to the door after it closed. "I don't."

The day passed in a fog, holding her brain hostage and refusing to release it, even for a moment. It took concentrated effort to get through the simplest of things. She felt as if she were sleepwalking through Shayne's clinic. Alison didn't know what to do about the feelings that were all knotted up inside. She wanted to be with Luc in every sense of the word, but at the same time she was afraid to be with him. Afraid of freezing. Worse, afraid of being afraid of freezing.

It was best not to get involved with him in the first place.

Too late, the phrase mocked her. She was there already, in the middle, or close to it. What she needed was a road map to show her how to get back outside again. Back to where things were just what they seemed and fun meant listening to hours worth of CDs.

"You look a little preoccupied."

Her eyes jerked up from what she was writing. Without thinking, she flipped the folder closed. Jacob was standing in front of the reception desk, not more than six inches away from her. She hadn't heard him come in. The clinic was supposed to be closed for lunch.

"Jacob, hi. I missed you both at breakfast today."

Sitting on the corner of her desk, he took the excuse in stride. "Luc said something about you needing to get an early start. I hope we're not driving you out."

The smile on his face was easygoing, genial. "No, of course not." She took a breath, collecting herself. Trying not to sound like a scatter-brained idiot. "I just didn't expect you here." And Shayne was out on a call. Nerves drummed through her.

She looked up at Jacob's face. He looked a little pale, but she'd assumed that was his normal color. "You're not sick, are you?"

"No, I'm actually feeling a lot healthier than I have in quite some time. I'm strictly playing errand boy." She flashed a grin. "Luc sent me to get you."

So, he didn't even want to come to pick her up. Could she blame him? She'd almost taken off his head this morning. And as for last night...

She pushed the file into the overflowing To Be Filed box. Maybe she'd come by later to catch up on that. Hearing about the picnic from Luc, Shayne had insisted on giving her the afternoon off. She owed him time. "It'll only take me a few minutes to get ready."

"No rush." Jacob got off the desk, stepping back and out of her way. "Gives me a chance to say a few words to you."

She slanted a look in his direction. Had Luc said something to him about her crazy behavior? "About?"

"Jean-Luc."

She released the breath she'd been holding. "What about him?"

"Just that I came back expecting to find..." How did he put this without making it sound insulting? "Well, whatever I expected to find, I didn't find it. Instead, I see that Luc's really happy. A large part of that's due to you."

She waved away his words. They had nothing to do with the truth. "I think you're giving me too much credit."

"No, I'm not." Jacob came around so that he could face her. "He was always an easygoing guy, happy with whatever he had. But when—" He stopped, flushing. "I guess you know the circumstances surrounding the three of us." She merely nodded in reply, allowing him to continue. "When Janice left him and then married me, well, I was afraid that was the end of our friendship. Worse, I was afraid that Luc would never come around again as far as relationships went. For the first time in my life, I'm really glad to be wrong."

Taking her hand in his, Jacob looked at her for a long moment, then added, "If the road gets bumpy up ahead, give him a little slack. He's a really great guy."

"Yes," she answered quietly, drawing her hands away. "I know."

"All set?"

She nodded, taking her purse. "All set."

But that was far from true.

The sky, framing a pristine mountain range that picturesquely still retained some of its snow, seemed endless. Endless and crystal-blue.

"I forgot how beautiful it was out here," Jacob said.

His head cradled in his wife's lap, he lay in the grass just staring at the sky. "How peaceful." By the sound of his voice, a laziness was beginning to slip through him. "I'm really going to miss this place when I go back."

"Right." Sitting on one side of the red-checkered tablecloth he'd purloined for the afternoon from the Salty, Luc laughed. "You can't take more than three days of peace and quiet in a row without looking as if you're about to go crazy."

"Maybe," Jacob conceded, "but it's still nice having someplace to go to unwind."

"We could look into that cabin the Andersons are selling. It's close to home," Janice reminded him, home being Los Angeles.

"Yes, but there're roots here." Jacob sounded wistful. Then, as if hearing himself, he squeezed her hand. "Don't worry, I'll sell the old homestead." He knew that was what she was worried about. That he'd find an excuse to hang on to it.

"Why?"

It was Alison who posed the question, and they all turned to look at her.

Janice frowned at her. "Because that's why we came. To sell his parents' property."

"But why sell it?" Alison prodded. She rose on her knees, enthusiasm getting the better of her. The idea she was toying with seemed like a nice way around everything. "Why not turn it into something? Some kind of business?" She turned to Luc, looking for backup. "You're good at that sort of thing. Can't the house be turned into something? A sort of bed-and-breakfast-type hotel, maybe?" Work on the hotel that already existed, Sydney had told her, had been at a standstill for almost two years now. The money and interest on the owner's part had long since run out and it remained now like an incomplete thought, standing in the shadows of the town. "People do come through in the summer, Shayne told me so." She'd even had a tourist or two pointed out to her. "Maybe they'd stay a while if there was somewhere *to* stay."

Jacob rolled the idea over in his head. The more he did, the more he liked it. "She might have something there."

"Sure I do. It wouldn't take much work. Just a little carpentry."

She probably had no idea how adorable she looked when she was being enthusiastic, Luc thought. "What do you know about carpentry?"

Now she was talking strictly to him. In a way, this breached the gap caused by the words they'd had this morning.

"Enough. My brothers were always fooling around with power tools, building on to the house. Kevin and I worked on the room you slept in above the garage," she told him proudly. "I'm a lot handier with a drill than I am with a skillet."

Luc had a sudden image of her wearing only a tool belt and had to curb the grin that came to his lips.

"You slept over her garage?" Janice looked at him curiously. "When did this happen?"

Too late she remembered she wasn't supposed to elaborate on the past and inadvertently throw a wrench into whatever tale he'd told them about her.

"Long story," Alison said quickly, waving it away. "But I am handy. Probably half the people here are handy." She saw the highly amused look exchanged between Luc and Jacob. "What? What did I say?"

"You obviously never told her about the house raisings we've had around here," Jacob surmised.

"Well, there you go," Alison declared, glad that was solved. "Now you don't have to sell."

But Jacob wasn't completely convinced, even though he wanted to be. "Who's going to run this so-called hotel?"

"Details, just details," Luc told him easily. "They'll take care of themselves in time. They always do."

Translation, he'd take care of them, Alison thought. Something akin of pride filtered through her as she looked at Luc.

"Okay," Jacob allowed. "I'll hold you to that."

"Jacob—" Janice began to protest.

He took her hand and brought it to his lips. "Let me work this out on my own. I think we might have the perfect solution here."

Janice merely shrugged, knowing when to back away.

"That was pretty sharp of you today," Luc told Alison in their room later that evening, after Jacob and Janice had gone to bed. "Coming up with turning the old house into a hotel." He undid the buttons of his shirt as he talked, trying his best to seem nonchalant. Holding his breath as to her reaction. "I don't think Jacob really wanted to sell it. Getting rid of it was Janice's idea." Making money always was. *There but for the grace of God...* "Now that you showed her there was profit to be made in keeping the old place, she's not against keeping it anymore."

As with any compliment, she shrugged it away. "Glad I could help."

He saw the set of her shoulders as she turned from him. It was happening again. But this time he wasn't going to ignore it, wasn't going to hope it would resolve itself without any intervention on his part. He owed it to her to intervene.

His shirt hanging open, he moved around her until they were face-to-face. "Alison, I don't want you to think that you have anything to be afraid of from me."

The defiance that had always seen her through was quick to rise. "I'm not afraid of you."

He hadn't meant that to sound like a challenge of some sort. "Not me, exactly, but something about me." He saw the denial begin to form. "Don't lie to me, Alison. It's there in your eyes. I just wish…"

She bunched her pajamas up against her, turning the doorknob to the bathroom. "Yeah, me, too."

When she came out of the bathroom fifteen minutes later, Luc was on the floor. He'd made a pallet for himself beside the four-poster. She set her clothing down on the chair beside the bureau.

"What are you doing?"

He glanced in her direction. As if he hadn't heard her come out. "Getting ready for bed."

She ran her brush through her hair, trying vainly to keep her mind on what she was doing. She lost count after three. "It's your bed. If anyone belongs on the floor, it's me."

"You're right. It is my bed and I get to decide who sleeps in it." He glanced at her, then went back to smoothing out the blanket. "My decision is that it's you."

Still holding the hairbrush, she crouched down beside him. Their eyes met. Her mouth curved. "This is ridiculous—you know that, don't you?"

He smiled in response. "I make it a practice never to argue with a lady."

The sigh that escaped her lips seemed to empty her completely. With her back against his bed, Alison eased down beside him. "It wasn't you last night."

He tried to keep it light, thinking it might make it easier on her. "Felt like me."

"I mean…" She was diving into deep waters, waters she wasn't sure if she knew how to navigate. "I wanted to make love with you. It wasn't the alcohol. The alcohol only kept me from stopping myself."

"Otherwise you would have?"

"Otherwise I couldn't have." There was a difference. And there was more. "You would have stopped it. I mean, you would have sensed something wrong and turned away from me. And I didn't want that."

"Is that what he did? Derek? Did he turn away from you?" How badly had her marriage scarred her? From the looks of it, pretty badly.

She nodded. "Eventually." Alison dropped the hairbrush beside her. With her knees against her chest, she leaned her elbows on them and dragged both hands though her hair. "I can't really blame him."

No, and that was what set her apart, he thought. "Then why are you blaming yourself?"

The question roused her. Alison looked at him, confused. "What?"

"That's what you're doing. Blaming yourself for whatever it was that started all this." And it was eating her up.

She shook her head. "You don't know what you're talking about."

"Then tell me," he urged. "Tell me what I'm talking about, Alison." When she began to get up, he caught her hands in his, holding on. "I need to know. Let me in, Alison. I swear I won't hurt you."

The fight, the defensiveness within her, was beginning to wane. "I know you won't. At least, you won't mean to, but..." Biting her lip, she looked off.

He sighed. "Have it your way. I won't pressure you, Alison. We'll do this at your pace." With that, he lay down on the floor and wrapped the comforter around himself, his back to her.

Alison sat there beside him, looking at Luc's back for a long time. Thinking. Wrestling. Maybe it was because she thought he was asleep that she even had enough courage to whisper, "I was too afraid to say anything. When it happened, I was too afraid."

He turned around slowly, not sure if he'd imagined hearing her. One look at her face told him he hadn't. Without a word he took her into his arms and just held her.

Alison felt something hitch in her throat. Tears, fighting to block her words. But suddenly she needed to get rid of them. Needed to have someone hear. And maybe tell her it was all right.

"I was...I was eleven." Every word felt as if she was running razor blades along her tongue. "My father had just died and I guess I was really scared. Scared about the future, scared about Kevin dying, too. He was like another father to me. I'd already lost my mother three years earlier so I was one parent short, and then Daddy died...." Her voice caught. It took a moment before she could continue. "So I was scared. That was when Uncle Jack started coming around. Right after my Dad's car accident. To see that everything was all right. To help out."

Luc tightened his arm around her, somehow knowing what was coming. Wishing that holding her would make the words come out differently.

"Kevin and Jimmy thought he was a great guy. So did I. He wasn't my real uncle, just my father's best friend. Uncle Jack had always been around, so we didn't think...I didn't think..." She took a deep breath. It shuddered its way into her lungs. "When he touched me, I got so scared."

Anger flared. "The son of a bitch—"

She couldn't let herself acknowledge Luc's comment. She'd break down if she did. So she caught her lip to keep from crying, forcing the words out instead. "But he said it was all right, that it was just because I was so pretty and he loved pretty girls. He said that what he was doing wouldn't hurt. That he'd never hurt me—"

Words he'd said to her, Luc realized. How had that affected her? Had it triggered more painful memories? "Oh, Alison, I'm so sorry."

She shut her eyes, tears squeezing through the lashes. "I stopped eating, stopped going to school. Kevin didn't know what to do with me. He thought it was because Dad was gone. And then one day, he heard me crying. I was in the closet. Praying and asking God to forgive me for making Jack do what he did. I'd never seen Kevin so pale. He made me tell him. Everything." Her control shredding, she looked at Luc. "Kevin's the only one who ever knew all the details. I thought he was going to kill Uncle Jack with his bare hands. Two of his friends had to pull him off."

There was nothing Luc could do but stroke her hair and hold her. He'd never felt so impotent in his life. Or so furious. "What did the police have to say?"

She shook her head. "Kevin didn't call them. He didn't want to put me all through that, telling strangers about what had happened. Being cross-examined by someone Jack would pay to twist everything back to me.

It was all moot, anyway. Jack disappeared right after that. Nobody ever knew what happened to him. Everybody talked about what a great guy he was and that they couldn't understand what made him take off.'' Her head resting against Luc's shoulder, she blew out a shaky breath. ''I thought it was my fault. What he did, his leaving. All of it. My fault.''

That was ridiculous. Luc bit back the retort. Instead, he kept his voice calm, mild, all the while empathizing with the rage Kevin must have felt. ''How could it have been your fault that that worthless scum molested you?''

She closed her eyes, remembering with a clarity that was almost frightening every single feeling she'd experienced. ''Because if I hadn't been there—''

He raised her chin until she opened her eyes and looked at him.

''He would have preyed on another little girl. Those kind of people are sick, Alison, no matter how nice they seem to be. They're like those shiny red apples that are rotten inside when you bite into them. Nobody suspects anything until they go beneath the top layer.''

''Maybe,'' she allowed.

''Maybe nothing. You weren't to blame. Aren't to blame,'' he emphasized fiercely, then lowered his voice. ''Did you ever tell your husband?''

That, too, was her fault. ''No.''

''Didn't he suspect anything was wrong?'' He couldn't see how the man could have possibly remained in the dark, not when he himself had suspected something was wrong almost from the start.

There was a sad smile on her lips. ''When I wouldn't have sex with him while we were still going together, I told him I was saving myself for the right guy. He was thrilled that it was him. He wasn't so thrilled afterward, though. He thought I was using sex as some kind of a bargaining chip. He lost patience with me pretty fast. Told me I was frigid, that there was something wrong with me. I shouldn't have married him.''

"Why did you?" he asked softly.

At the time her reasoning had seemed right. It was only now that she saw how flawed it had been. "To prove to myself that I was all right. That I could move on. I thought that if I was married, those dreams wouldn't haunt me anymore.'' Another miscalculation. "They just got worse.''

"Dreams?"

"Of Uncle Jack." She shuddered even as she said it. "Of his hands reaching out for me, or his breath surrounding me. He smoked. To this day, I smell a cigarette, I start to choke.'' She looked down. "I'm sorry, you don't need to be hearing this.''

He wasn't going to have her turning away from him. Not after she'd just shared her darkest secret with him. "But I do. How can I help if I don't know?''

She turned into the safety his arms provided. "And how are you going to help?''

"By being there when you feel you need someone. By being there even when you don't.'' He looked into her eyes, silently making a pledge to her. "By doing whatever you need to get you through the night.''

And then he kissed her.

Chapter Fifteen

This time there was nothing to hide behind. No excuses, no false courage to take the fall for what she felt.

This time, as she felt the pull that Luc's touch along her body generated, felt the yearning begin within her, there was nothing to protect her. Nothing to point to and blame her actions on.

The desire was of her own making.

As was the passion.

Alison knew what awaited her, and even though her fear of the devastating fear still hovered somewhere just beyond, it was not as deep, not as thick, not as solid as before. A glimmer of white light shone through it, showing her the way. Whispering promises of salvation.

He deepened the kiss. She felt his tongue touch hers, felt his arms tighten around her as he brought her even closer.

A euphoria overtook her, too large to be ignored, too

wide to be contained. Wrapping her arms around his neck, she leaned her body into his, absorbing the warm, comforting feel of it.

Absorbing it and reveling in it.

She was like sunlight in his hands, like moonbeams and dreams. He couldn't quite believe that it was happening twice.

There was a difference to her this time from the last. This time, there was no wild push to reach journey's end; she seemed to be savoring the steps it took to get there. Luc felt his heart swelling, quickening. He wanted to give her the moon, to give her every pleasure ever created beneath it.

Slowly the layers peeled away. Layers of clothing, layers of protection that kept them safe from the world. Insulated from one another.

Neither one of them wanted to be safe tonight, unless it was with the other.

He didn't ask her this time if she was sure. He knew—sensed—she was. This time there was no part of him that stood back, waiting for a sign that she wanted to pull away, that she was regretting what she'd allowed to begin. There were no shackles, no checks. All there was was a purity of yearning. Of innocence revisited, because, despite everything, she was innocent in what a man and a woman could do when heaven and earth were right.

He wanted to show her how it could be. To pleasure her and to leave her with feelings that were strong enough, stirring enough, to block out all of the bad that had happened to her. Block it out as if it had never happened at all.

He made love not only with her, but to her. To every part of her, however small.

He kissed her fingertips, drawing them one by one slowly into his mouth until he heard her whimper with desire, with anticipation. He pressed a kiss to each palm, to her arms, to the expanse above her breasts, circling each slowly so that he tantalized her and tortured himself before his tongue finally touched each peak. Moistening. Suckling.

Making sensations scramble helter-skelter through her, bouncing here, there. Everywhere.

Alison arched against his mouth, freely giving herself up to him, to the pleasures that were battering so urgently at every part of her. She grasped the blankets beneath her as his mouth went lower, laying claim first to her belly, then christening the path that led him further on his quest.

When his tongue came in contact with the very core of her, she bit down hard to keep from crying out. The cry echoed within her body instead.

And then, when the first of the climaxes hit, she spiraled completely up to another level. Damp with perspiration, she could only cleave to a hope that there was more. A greediness overtook her.

She couldn't get her fill of him.

She'd never known it could be like this. Never suspected that she was capable of feeling these sort of sensations, and be filled with a desire to give back at least a small measure of what she was experiencing. She wanted him to feel as insanely happy as she was right at this moment.

There was a unity here, a unity that took her breath away and made her want to sing and sob with joy at the same time.

Her breath coming in short, shallow snatches, Alison

caught hold of his shoulders, urging him up to her, wanting to see his eyes, touch his face.

Wanting him.

The first time had been wonderful, but this, this broke through a door, destroying its locks, bending its hinges so that it could never again be closed.

Never again close off the light and keep it from reaching her again.

He'd set her free.

Luc felt as if his heart had stopped. There were tears in her eyes. Had he hurt her? Had he done something after all that brought all those terrible memories back to her?

"Alison…"

"Shh."

She placed the tips of her fingers to his lips, silencing him. This wasn't the time for words, only feelings. Only actions.

And then, because he wasn't expecting it, she managed to rise and twist so that she switched places with him. He became the one on his back, he was the one under sensual assault as she at first timidly, and then with more and more surety, put into practice what he had taught her.

How to make love.

Arrows tipped in fire shot through him, searing him wherever her tongue touched him. Nearly sending him over the brink.

The feel of her lips—eager, curved, sensual—rained fleeting openmouthed kisses over his hardened torso, quickening his pulse throughout all the points where it beat. Making him crazy.

Making him desire her beyond a point where all rational thoughts converged.

It would have taken a stronger man than he to resist, to hold back indefinitely. Feeling the pressure, the demands of his weakening body, he took hold of her shoulders and gently drew her back to him.

He was stopping her. Her lips were throbbing, her eyes not quite able to focus as she looked at him. Had she done it wrong? "Don't you like it?"

"That's just the trouble," he breathed. "I like it too much."

His lips crushed against hers as Luc tightened his arms around her, holding her to him, kissing her to a state of senselessness as he reversed their positions.

And then he entered her. Entered before the explosion that was threatening to unleash racked his body. Using the last of his control, he began the rhythm slowly. But the urgency that had shadowed their every movement was here, as well, and strong. The final pleasure was not long in coming.

It held him tightly in its grip before allowing him to slowly regain his foothold on earth. Contentment circled around him like papal white smoke, signifying peace and a new beginning.

He loved her.

Like words written across the sky, riding on a lightning bolt, it came to him.

He loved her.

In keeping his feelings safe within this charade, he'd been free to let them come. To grow. He'd allowed himself to pretend to go through the motions of everything he longed for. He played the part with conviction—until the player had become lost in the role and the lines between reality and make-believe had become completely blurred.

Reality had superseded make-believe.

He loved her and he hadn't a clue what to do about it. Because the last time he'd loved, it had been snatched away from him, leaving him standing with nothing but his heart in his hands. Empty.

He didn't want that happening again, didn't want that feeling to become part of his life again.

He loved her.

He wasn't going to think about that now, Luc told himself. For now it was enough just to hold her in his arms, to breathe in the scent of her and know that she was his for this space of time. It was more than he had a right to ask.

The warmth around her didn't abate, even after the contentment of lovemaking had faded into a cottony presence. She wanted to thank him for making the shadows go away. Wanted to tell him just how grateful she was for this liberation he'd provided.

She wanted to tell him how he made her feel. *That* he made her feel. And there was such a wealth of feelings within her. Especially happiness. It ricocheted through her like a specially crafted ball that went to unimaginable heights with each bounce.

But she knew how he'd felt about Janice, knew that Luc wasn't looking to be entangled with anyone. To tell him would be to take the magic away from both of them and bring only emptiness.

So she remained lying next to him, content to be held by this man who had liberated her. Content to feel his steady breath along her skin and to let the night, such as it was, come.

Because she wasn't afraid anymore. He was with her and she couldn't ask for more than that.

She was gone.

The place beside him was empty. Cool to the touch

when he reached for her. Just like the first morning after he'd spent with her. His eyes flew open even as the thought penetrated.

Memories of another time, another empty bed, came flooding back to him.

"Alison?" he called. Not waiting for a reply, he got up and quickly pulled on his jeans. He ignored his shoes. "Alison?"

There was no answer. It was unreasonable, but he couldn't shake the concern that was gripping his heart. He hurried out into the hall. "Alison?"

Jacob opened the door of the room he was sharing with Janice. Confused, he looked at Luc, bleary-eyed. "Who's Alison?"

Distracted, telling himself that this wasn't déjà vu and that he had nothing to worry about, Luc turned toward Jacob. Explanations that were nothing more than coated lies came to his tongue, but then he thought better of them. The time for lies had passed.

"Jake, I've got something to tell you."

Jacob sat at the kitchen table, nursing the mug of inky black coffee Luc had poured for him. Some of it was already in his veins so that he was able to comprehend what was being said to him.

Hearing Luc out, he could only ·shake his head. "Well, if she's not your wife, then what the hell are you waiting for?"·

The question had nothing to do with the confession he'd just given him. Luc had expected humor, or even a question as to why he'd felt the deception necessary to undertake. He set down his own empty mug on the counter and picked up the pot of freshly brewed coffee. He was still trying to set his fears to rest.

"What do you mean?"

"I mean, ask her to marry you." Jacob saw the startled look on Luc's face and couldn't believe the thought hadn't crossed his friend's mind. "Any woman who'd follow you up to this godforsaken wilderness—and you know it is, for the most part—and then pretend to be your wife just so that you could supposedly save face, well, it has to mean she cares about you. Marry the woman already."

Luc sighed. Jacob always had a habit of plowing into the center of things without regards to the perimeters. "It's not that simple." He poured the coffee, then took a drink. "There're complications."

Jacob pushed his mug forward on the counter, silently asking for it to be topped off. "Get rid of them."

Luc laughed shortly as he did the honors. Same old Jacob. "Easy for you to say."

"Yeah, easy, because I live by it." He raised his mug in a silent toast to the edict that had governed most of his adult life. "I want something, I find a way to get it. I'm hell to live with until I do. Ask Janice." He took a long swig of his coffee. "The way I see it, the woman loves you."

Maybe he had even nurtured that hope himself, but hearing it said out loud showed Luc how ludicrous that thought was. Especially in light of what she had told him last night. She was afraid to love.

So what was *last night about?*

He waved a hand at Jacob. "You don't know what you're talking about."

"None so blind as those who refuse to see," he murmured. "As for me, I've got eyes, don't I? I see the way that woman looks at you. With affection—and something more." He paused, wrestling with the wisdom of what he wanted to say. Deciding it was for the best, he forged ahead. "Janice never looked at you like that, you know." He saw the surprise in Luc's eyes and nodded. "Yes, I used to watch the two of you, too. She was the one thing I never went out for—until I was sure I wasn't breaking the two of you up."

Luc leaned across the counter. This was something he hadn't realized before. "But you were in love with her."

"From the third grade." He grinned, finishing his coffee. "I've got a sense about these things. Just like I have a sense about you and—what's her name, Alison?" Luc nodded. "Pretty name. Prettier girl. Want my advice, put your marker down, Jean-Luc, before one of those scruffy miners beats you to it. Gold doesn't get passed up around here. And that woman's pure gold."

He'd never been a coward about anything before. This wouldn't be the time to start, Luc told himself. He finished his own coffee before answering. "First I've got to find her."

No-brainer, Jacob thought. "She's probably at work. She said something to Janice yesterday about feeling guilty, leaving all those files piling up at the clinic." He smiled in admiration. "She's got a powerful work ethic. If I wasn't already married, I'd go after her myself."

"Oh, no, not this time."

It was a joke, but Jacob didn't kid himself. There was an underlying steel wire of truth in the warning. "Don't worry. Janice and I have our ups and downs, but as far as I can tell, we're perfect for each other. Just like you and Suzanne—I mean Alison."

The sudden pounding on the front door interrupted anything further that could have been said.

* * *

Considering her lack of sleep, she was incredibly energetic.

She'd hardly slept at all.

Alison had felt too wired, too happy to fall asleep last night. It had been all she could do to keep from singing.

This morning, though, was another story. She hadn't stopped humming and singing under her breath since she'd left the house. She'd crept out of bed early, careful not to wake Luc. Careful not to mar the aura that last night had created.

Determined to catch up on the work she'd allowed to pile up, Alison had arrived at the clinic before Shayne. She was going to need more time off and she didn't want to feel badly about it, even though Shayne had told her that she could take all the time she needed. Visitors weren't exactly commonplace in Hades.

Maybe that would change with the hotel. Jacob had given every indication of wanting to utilize her idea. Even Janice had come around, as long as she knew she didn't have to remain in Hades to see the project through.

She didn't see why the woman hated it so. Hades had a lot going for it if one's main focus in life wasn't getting all the latest cable channels.

Picking up another armload of files, she moved to the next filing bin. Janice and Jacob were leaving tomorrow and she wanted to go with Luc to see them off.

Leaving. The thought brought a slight frown to her lips, halting the song she was singing. This was going to be her last night with Luc as his "wife." Tomorrow, Jacob and Janice would be gone and with them the need for any kind of pretense.

Would Luc still want to see her after this? Would what had been started behind closed bedroom doors abruptly end, as well? She wished she knew. She'd opened her heart to him last night and now she didn't want that to change.

But she couldn't very well come out and talk to him about that even though she didn't like hanging back. She'd always taken the proverbial bull by the horns rather than adopt a wait-and-see attitude. But she couldn't ask him what the future held for them after his friends boarded the plane. That would be putting pressure on him and she knew how men were about pressure.

This was going to be frustrating as hell, she thought, but there was nothing she could do about it.

Maybe he was even glad the charade was going to be over. He'd already mentioned that he didn't like carrying on the pretense. Another man would have used it to his benefit, to keep her in his bed.

But Luc wasn't another man and that was why she loved him.

"What are you doing here so early?"

She didn't jump, she realized a second after she turned around to look at Shayne in the doorway. Feeling like a person in the throes of a magical cure, she indicated the files. "I thought I'd catch up on what I left behind yesterday."

Woman was one in a million, he thought. Shayne slipped on his lab jacket. "Remind me to thank Luc again."

She paused, her fingers holding her place between Smythe and Smurmir. "For what?"

"For you." He unlocked the cabinet where he kept his supply of prescription medication. "All those endless months of beating the bushes, trying to find a nurse to come up here, all I can say is, you were certainly worth waiting for."

She'd always been a hard worker, but she'd never been one to garner praise. Maybe because she'd never been one to know how to accept it graciously. That, too, was about to change, she told herself. "You make it hard to think about leaving."

The words froze him in his tracks. "Are you? Thinking about leaving?"

She slipped Esra Poole's file into its place. "Well, when my internship is over, I'd have to decide if—"

Shayne didn't let her get any further. Experience had taught him to nip things in the bud. "I've never resorted to bribery before, but whatever it takes to keep you here, I'll get it for you or steal it for you. And if I can't, Ike can. I'd ask Luc to do it since you two are closer, but if they ever created a man more honest than him, I've never met him."

Not that she wasn't about to sing his praises, but it seemed that Shayne was overlooking something very basic here. "He lied about being married."

Shayne knew all about that. Ike had told him the circumstances surrounding the lie. Now that he thought of it, it was fortunate for all of them that Luc had lied. Otherwise, she might never have come here to them.

"That was just an unfortunate misunderstanding." Shayne took his instruments out of the container where he sterilized them. "He did it under the influence of a few drinks too many."

She thought of her own first foray into lovemaking with Luc. "I guess things happen when we let our guard down."

There was something in her voice that gave Shayne pause. As private as Luc, perhaps even more so, he debated how far to venture. These were friends and the rules changed for friends.

"You know, Sydney says I have to be hit over the head with a moose before I notice the oncoming, stampeding herd. But if it's not butting in too much, I would like to say that I've noticed a change in Luc lately. This charade the two of you have been caught up in seems to have taken root."

Her brows drew together in confusion. "What do you mean?"

How did he put this? "There's a certain spring to Luc's step whenever you're around." The assessment sounded incredibly corny to his ear, but it was true.

Alison stopped filing. The edge of Jason Evers's file wrinkled as she clutched it between her thumb and forefinger. "Do you think?"

"I think."

And then the front door of the clinic slammed against the opposite wall as someone pushed it open. "Shayne!"

"Back here, Ike."

Alison caught her breath when she saw him. Ike was dirty, with dust and soot on his clothes and face.

"What the hell happened to you?"

The answer wasn't direct. "Shayne, bring your medical bag. There's been a cave-in at the mine. At least fifteen men have been hurt and there're still some trapped inside. I've sent out the alarm for every able-bodied male in the area."

A single thought came to Alison. *Luc!*

Chapter Sixteen

It amazed her how quickly her heart could launch itself into her throat. Alison was at Ike's side instantly. "Is Luc there?"

"Probably by now. I sent Yuri to get him. Yuri's pretty shook up," Ike told Shayne. He was talking to the latter's back as Shayne quickly went to the medical supply cabinet and gathered together what he felt he'd need at the site. "He was supposed to go in today, but he was sleeping off a hangover in the back room when we heard about the cave-in. We figure a minor earthquake might have triggered it."

Shayne turned around, closing his bag. "How bad is it?"

"Bad." It was the first time Alison had ever seen a grim expression on Ike's face and it chilled her down to the bone. "I don't know if we can dig them all out. It looks like one of the main bracing structures just gave way. We won't know until we clear everything and get inside. But that could be days.''

Or longer, Alison thought.

Ready to leave, Shayne looked at Alison. "Think you can handle the clinic on your own?''

Shayne's question pulled her up short. It hadn't occurred to her that she'd be remaining behind. The clinic wasn't due to open for at least half an hour yet. "Couldn't I go with you? You might need the help,'' she tagged on, hoping it would sway him.

In response, Shayne glanced at Ike. Ike nodded grimly. "Couldn't hurt.''

Shayne opened the front door for her. "All right, Alison, let's go.''

She didn't remember crossing the floor.

She didn't remember the trip there, either. It was as if she was suspended above time and space. Nothing registered. All she could think of was what if somehow, something happened to Luc while he was trying to help rescue the miners. She knew he wouldn't hang back or put his own safety above that of others. That wasn't in his nature.

She wanted to tell him things, so many things, pour out the contents of her heart. But there was no time.

Oh, please let there be time.

She sat on the edge of her seat the entire way.

The Halliday Mine was located five miles out of the center of town. Close enough for a determined miner to walk to the Salty if his thirst was strong enough, far away enough so most of the noise involved in running a mine didn't bother the local residents who lived in the town proper.

The scene at the mine looked like the heart of a storm.

Chaos was ensuing as men were hurrying to and fro, trying their best to handle this unexpected curve that nature had thrown them. There hadn't been a cave-in at the mine for over ten years.

More than fifteen injured men lay on the ground, made as comfortable as possible under the circumstances by their comrades. The ones who had gotten out in one piece were trying to dig out the others who hadn't been so lucky. The cave-in had been destructively thorough, taking out the gaping mouth of the cave and reducing it to barely a leering crack.

Quickly climbing out of the vehicle, her heart pounding, Alison lost no time in looking for Luc. Ike was right behind her.

She found Luc, along with Jacob, trying to clear the entrance.

It looked almost impossible without machinery to help them, but the Bobcat used to shovel large rocks away, Ike had told her, was down and inoperable.

Relief washed over her when she saw Luc. She saw surprise in his eyes. "What are you doing here? Don't you know it's dangerous?"

"I could say the same thing to you."

There was no time to waste arguing. All he could do was shake his head.

"Can't you blast them away?" Alison gestured toward the haphazard wall of rocks.

Luc raked his hand through his hair, frustrated. "Not without knowing what it's like inside the mine. Any kind of blast might cause more cave-ins. Hennessey says the powder man's inside." He nodded toward the man for Ike's benefit.

Alison looked from Ike to Luc. "Powder man?"

Ike resumed his place amid the rubble and began removing rocks. "The man who knows just what kind of a charge to use and where to put it."

"There's nobody else?" She couldn't believe they'd have only one man who was knowledgeable about the process.

Luc stopped, considering. There were plenty of explosives on hand, there just wasn't anyone to put them to use. He wiped his hands on his jeans, looking at Ike. "I might be able to do it, but I'd still need to get inside first." He was aware of the stunned way Alison was looking at him. He couldn't help the grin that came to his lips. "Told you I did a lot of reading."

"Reading what?" she demanded, her heart beginning to constrict. "How to blow things up?"

"Books on how to operate a mine," he answered.

Luc saw the worry in her eyes. He wanted to talk to her, to tell her what he'd been thinking, what he'd felt this morning, waking up and not finding her there. He wanted to tell her that all he wanted out of this world was to find her there every morning for the rest of his life. But this wasn't the time or the place. There were men's lives to think of first.

Later he could pour out his heart.

Ike stared at the rubble, doing a little quick calculating. "If we all work together, we can probably clear away enough rocks to get you in at least part of the way."

Luc nodded. "That might be all it'll take."

What were they saying? A salvo of panic went straight to her belly. Alison grabbed Luc's arm, commandeering his attention. "You're not going in there?"

His eyes met hers, silently asking her to understand. "I've got no choice."

She didn't want to hear that. "Yes, you do. You've always got a choice."

His voice was low, calm. The calm within the center of the storm. "Alison, what if those were your brothers trapped in there?"

She couldn't argue with him. His point was taken. She knew she had no right to ask him not to do this. Even if their relationship was more binding, even if he was her husband and not just the man she suddenly knew she belonged with, she still had no right to have him turn his back on his conscience.

Dropping her hand, she nodded and stepped back. "If there's a chance, you have to go," she agreed quietly.

The next second, she felt him grab her by the shoulders and kiss her hard on the mouth.

"For luck," he told her, already hurrying away to get the explosives he was going to need.

It was only after she'd caught her breath that she realized he'd called her Alison in front of Jacob. The latter hadn't blinked an eye.

"You know?" she asked.

Jacob nodded. "Since this morning. He told me. Luc hates lying, always has." There was nothing but admiration in his voice. "Great guy."

There was no need to tell her that.

And then there was no time to say anything at all as more volunteers arrived to diligently try to clear away the rocks from where the mouth of the cave had once been.

Knowing she could be more help elsewhere, Alison turned away and hurried to find Shayne.

For the next hour, Alison moved from man to man in Shayne's wake, doing what she could to help. There were wounds to clean and bandage, broken limbs to temporarily set and judgment calls to make as to who was going to have to be airlifted to the hospital at Anchorage and who was just going to be sent home.

She worked tirelessly, not allowing herself to focus on anything except the injured man beneath her hands. She certainly couldn't allow herself to think about what could happen once Luc finally had clear access to the mine's interior.

"He's going in," someone called.

Alison slipped and poured too much alcohol onto the cotton swab, turning it into a soggy sponge. Dropping it to the ground, she hurried away from the miner whose wound she'd been cleaning. He'd been one of the lucky ones. Three cuts and a bruise, none of which required much attention.

"I'll be right back," she tossed over her shoulder.

"I'll be here." But the miner was saying it to her back.

Oblivious, Alison flew to where all of the commotion was originating.

The men had managed to clear away enough of an opening for Luc, a flashlight and the explosives he was bringing to squeeze through. Two feet by two feet.

It didn't seem nearly enough room to squeeze in her whole world, she thought.

Tears of panic filled her eyes. She blinked them back, determined not to cry. That was for later, when he came back to her. Without thinking, Alison clutched at Ike's arm.

Moving it, he silently slipped his arm around her shoulders in mute encouragement.

There had to be another way, there just had to. "I'm smaller," she heard herself saying to Ike. "I could crawl in there and—"

He knew that desperation rather than logic was goading her to make the offer. "That's just the point. You are smaller," Ike told her. "Too small to drag out a man, especially if he's injured. And unless you know your way around explosives—" Defeated, she shook her head. Ike gave her shoulder a quick, reassuring squeeze. "He's going to be all right."

"Sure he is," she murmured. She only wished she could believe it herself.

It was as if time stood still. Certainly her breath had, lodging itself in her lungs as she stared at the mine's opening, willing Luc to emerge again.

Every noise, every faint rumble whether from the vicinity of the mine or not, had her heart stopping, as well. Stopping and then beating wildly. Hard enough so that she felt as if her head was spinning.

Damn it, where was *he? Why hadn't he come out by now? What if—?*

She wouldn't let herself go there.

When she finally saw someone coming out of the opening, she felt like crying out for joy. But a moment later, the joy faded. It wasn't Luc.

"Hey, it's Riley," someone shouted.

The man, no more than twenty, looked visibly shaken and shaky. A woman cried out with relief as she came running toward him. Alison assumed it was his mother.

"Luc got me out," Thomas Riley told the man who took his arm to help support him. "I was pinned under this beam. Thought I was dead for sure."

Alison pushed forward through the clustered throng. "Where is he?"

"Back there," Riley answered weakly. "There're two more guys down there. Sawyer and Crenshaw. Behind some rock. Luc said he was going to give me five minutes to find my way out and then try to set a charge so that he can get to them.''

Everyone knew the risk that was implied. Unless set exactly right, there was a very good chance that none of them would be coming out. Any miscalculation could be fatal.

A fresh wave of panic clutched at her throat.

''Isn't there anything we can do?'' Alison pleaded with Ike.

Frustration clawed at him, as well. ''Praying comes to mind.''

She felt so stymied, so frustrated she could scream.

She needed to be doing something, making something happen. Digging her way to him with her bare hands, not just standing and staring at the cave, not knowing if she was standing on top of Luc's tomb.

Ike could see the turmoil in her eyes. ''Why don't you go back and help Shayne? It'll take your mind off this.''

It was too late for that. She shook her head. ''Nothing's going to take my mind off this,'' she whispered quietly.

She stayed where she was, hoping that Shayne would understand. She couldn't wrap her mind around anything else, except for what was happening right now beneath the ground.

Ike held her hand tightly and felt her nails sink into his flesh when the blast came. He heard her stifled cry.

Smoke belched out of the opening the miners and volunteers had cleared and they felt the ground beneath them shudder and tremble. It felt like another earthquake, a localized one.

As if possessed of a single thought, the men converged around the mouth again and began trying to clear away the remaining rocks. Alison was right there with them, taking her place beside Ike, working as fast as she could.

Drenched in fear, Alison began praying.

She prayed that that hadn't been an earthquake and that Luc would come back to her so she could tell him what was in her heart.

Keep him safe, God, and bring him back to me.

She'd never prayed so hard in her life.

More than five minutes went by. Five minutes in which everyone was digging and no one was talking, afraid of blotting out even the smallest of sounds coming from inside the mine. Afraid of somehow missing the one telltale noise that might signal a rescue.

And then a hand pushed through the newly created opening.

Men scrambled to grasp it, while others continued dragging rocks aside.

Alison was afraid to hope. Afraid not to hope.

A minute later, covered with dust from head to foot, Luc came stumbling out half dragging one man while another followed in his wake. All three were gasping for air and coughing.

The moment he surrendered the man he was supporting to someone else, Alison launched herself at Luc. Wrapping her arms around him, she kissed his mouth hard, ignoring the dust that covered his body and the grinning stares of the men around them.

Ignoring everything except that Luc was alive and had come back to her.

"Oh, God, Luc, are you hurt?" Worried now that she might have been squeezing an injured rib, she quickly ran her hands along his body as Shayne came forward.

Trying to catch his breath, Luc managed to look at

her. His stare was blank. "Luc? Who's Luc? And who are you? Do I know you?"

For one horrible moment, she thought he had amnesia again. But then she saw the gleam in his eye as he said, "I'm going to have to kiss you again. Maybe that'll jar something in my memory."

"I'll jar your memory all right." Laughing, she slipped her arms around his neck again. Her heart felt as if it was brimming over. "I'm so glad to see you, I'm not even going to kill you for putting me through that. I'll wait until later."

The wobbly feeling that had draped over his body was beginning to recede. It had been touch-and-go for a few minutes in the mine. A few minutes in which he thought he wasn't getting out. Entertaining thoughts of his own mortality; what he regretted most was not having told her he loved her.

"Couldn't you kill me after the wedding?"

Her eyes widened. "What wedding?"

"Our wedding?"

It was in the form of a question because even now he wasn't sure of the outcome, of her answer. He'd made up his mind this morning after making his confession to Jacob that he was going to ask Alison to marry him. He was going to ask, but what if she said no?

After his experience in the mine, he knew he wasn't about to take no for an answer.

Alison stared at him, stunned. This seemed to come out of nowhere. She was afraid to let her heart absorb the words. Afraid because she wanted this so much.

She cocked her head, studying him. "Are you sure you're not experiencing amnesia?"

"I'm sure." He wiped his hand against his jeans before touching her cheek. "But if you say yes, I'm bound to experience a little euphoria. What do you say, Alison? You want to make an honest man out of me?''

''C'mon, Alison, say yes!'' someone in the crowd coached. ''Don't leave him hanging.''

She laughed at Luc's play on words. ''It's usually the woman who needs to be made honest.''

''In my case, it's me,'' he told her.

She grew serious. He'd made a lovely gesture, owning up to the truth. She knew what that had to have cost him. Nobody likes looking foolish. ''Jacob told me you made a clean breast of it. He knows we're not married.''

''Yet,'' Luc stipulated. His eyes made an eloquent plea.

Temptation hovered over her, urging her to accept. But this was said in the heat of the moment and she didn't want him regretting it once the dust had settled. It cost her, but she gave him every opportunity to recant.

''Luc, you just had a harrowing life-and-death experience. Don't say anything hasty you might regret.''

''If you don't marry him, you want to marry me?'' another one of the volunteers asked, only to have Ike shove him aside good-naturedly.

''Shut up and let them work this out,'' he ordered.

''I've never said anything hasty in my life,'' Luc told her. ''And I'm not going to regret it, now or ever. I made up my mind to ask you this morning, before I heard about the cave-in.'' He took her hands into his, holding them to his chest. ''I want you to stay here with me after your internship is over. I don't want you to go back to Seattle, Alison. If you go, what will I do with my heart?''

Her own heart caught in her throat, this time held there with happiness.

"Say yes already, darlin'," Ike urged her, unable to take this any longer. "You know you want to."

The smile in her heart rose into her eyes. "Yes, I know I want to."

Catching her up in his arms, Luc raised her up high before enveloping her in a warm, if dusty, embrace.

"You're all invited to the wedding," he announced to the crowd. And then he smiled down into her face. "But not to the honeymoon."

A chorus of moans echoed around them as he kissed her, but neither of them heard.

Epilogue

The butterflies that sailed by above her head just as she entered the tent where she was to dress had nothing on the ones that were breeding in her stomach. With wings that were at least a yard wide, they were flapping for all they were worth.

She'd been here before, on the threshold of marriage. But the last time had been riddled with fear and a sick feeling in the pit of her stomach that she was making a huge, horrible mistake.

That feeling was absent now. Instead, there was an excitement, an eagerness and yes, a colossal case of nerves.

What if she wasn't—?

But she would be, Alison silently swore to herself. She would be a good wife. Luc's wife. It had a lovely ring to it.

She glanced down at her hand. The antique band she'd

grown so accustomed to wearing in such a short time was gone from her finger. Luc would be giving it to her officially in just a little while.

Her finger might have felt as if there were something missing, but her heart didn't. For the first time since she could remember, her heart felt...fearless. *She* felt fearless. And so happy she could burst.

"You beam any harder and those people waiting out there are going to think they've got two suns instead of one," Sydney told her.

"Let 'em." Alison couldn't keep the sparkle out of her eyes. "This has been a long time in coming."

After a while, Kevin popped his head into the camping tent that Ike and Shayne had put up for her less than an hour ago. "Almost time, Aly."

And then he saw her, really saw her. His little sister looked radiant. All the secret fears he'd had about this whirlwind courtship and wedding vanished. He knew now what a proud father of the bride felt. "Oh, baby, you look beautiful."

Alison smoothed down the skirt of her mother's wedding gown. Lily had brought it in her suitcase. The first time she married, Alison had worn her own. A simple little thing she'd bought herself, a dress that could be reused. Looking back, it was as if she'd known the marriage was doomed from the start and that at least the dress could be salvaged out of the fiasco.

But this time she'd known she would get married in her mother's wedding gown. For luck. Forever.

She looked down at it now. "It does look pretty, doesn't it?"

"I wasn't talking about the dress." Kevin felt a tightness in his throat. "Does Luc know how damn lucky he is?"

With Sydney's help, Marta spread out the train behind Alison. "If incessant talking and bragging about Alison is any indication, I think he might suspect." She cocked her head, listening. "Uh-oh, I think I hear your husband starting his fancy fingering at the keyboard." She winked at Sydney. Kevin and Ike had brought Sydney's beloved piano out into the field so that Alison and Luc could have music when they said the fateful words that pledged them to each other.

Sydney paused to listen. She winked at Alison. "Sounds like 'The Wedding March' to me."

Kevin presented his arm to the bride. He told himself he wasn't going to cry. It would only embarrass Alison. But his eyes were smarting. "Ready?"

She took a deep breath. "Yes, I am."

They left the tent slowly, with Marta, Sydney and Lily marching down the makeshift aisle before her in the wildflower-strewn field. It was the only place large enough to accommodate all the people Luc had invited.

And then it was Alison's turn. Alison's turn to grab the brass ring.

Luc turned from the altar and watched her approach. He knew she was beautiful, had thought so from the moment he had looked up at her in that alley and thought she was an angel. But the sight of her now, holding herself like a queen and coming toward him, left his mouth dry. And his heart brimming.

And then she was beside him, with the reverend saying the words that would seal him to her in the eyes of the state, the church and all their friends and family. Putting into reality what had been true from the first moment they had been together.

"...And I now pronounce you husband and wife. You may—" The reverend stopped and laughed. Not waiting for the man's instruction, Luc had taken Alison into his arms and was kissing her. In the background, Shayne began playing "Moon River," just as Luc had instructed him to. "I see you're already moving on ahead."

And they intended to keep right on doing just that. For the rest of their lives.

* * * * *

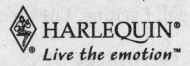

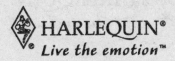

Harlequin Historicals®
Historical Romantic Adventure!

From rugged lawmen and valiant knights to defiant heiresses and spirited frontierswomen, Harlequin Historicals will capture your imagination with their dramatic scope, passion and adventure.

Harlequin Historicals . . . they're too good to miss!

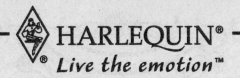

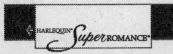